AN *Every Girl* NOVEL

NICOLE LOUFAS

ALEE

ISBN: 9780996494632

Copyright © 2019 by Nicole Loufas

www.nicoleloufas.com

Editing by Indie Solutions, www.murphyrae.net

Cover design by Murphy Rae, www.murphyrae.net

FOR MY ALI

IS OLD A SCENT?

Prologue

These pictures smell old. Their stench dances through the air every time my mother pulls the albums from their resting place. Her fingerprints smudge the worn plastic sheets, tarnishing them with sadness. Her tears seep into the pages, adding another layer of grief. She turns the page and winces at the memory trapped in the photo.

Why does she torture herself?

The little time capsule depicts a young, vibrant, hopeful woman. Nothing like the person sitting across the table. Traces of her tired brown eyes, sagging jowls, and overgrown eyebrows creep into my reflection. Just like the tiny lines forming around my eyes, I will inherit her grief. Her life is my destiny. Loss made it so.

We were loved once. Loved so completely. Loved in a way that could never be duplicated or replaced. When that love was gone, we surrendered to the sadness. We are alike in all the ways I do not want to be like her.

She sips from her crystal glass and stares into the next room. Her body is here, her mind is lost in a parallel dimension. A world where her dreams are reality. I wonder if I'm there too. Am I part of her dreams or am I only here, in the nightmare?

HAWK

Chapter One

TODAY

Superficial sadness is expressed with emojis and hashtags. Missing your bus, losing a parking space, your favorite bakery running out of scones—everyday life. There is no emoji for true grief. I'm talking about inexorable sorrow. Sorrow is like being shot with a gun. You'll never know how much it hurts until it happens to you.

After careful consideration, I opt not to comment on the post of girl I barely knew from middle school who lost her dog to cancer. Not because I don't like her or don't sympathize. I can't find the right emoji. With a simple flick of my index finger, the post rolls away. *RIP, Cooper.*

The crowded train rumbles into the station with a warning blast of the horn. It slows, then jolts to a stop. Passengers sway like slabs of beef as they cling to the metal bar that runs above the seats. I tuck my iPhone safely into my pocket before standing. San Francisco may be famous for cable cars and bridges but I know the real city. The callous and cold streets where a desperate junkie with one shoe, will snatch a phone right out of your hand, and dare to take it back. Today, I'm not in the mood to fight.

I step out of the 24th and Mission BART station with my eyes to the ground and start towards home. I learned early on not to make eye contact with the creeps who sit along the concrete wall behind the station. Politeness is seen as an opening to talk, an opportunity to ask for money, or to offer you twenty bucks to see your tits. A polite smile and fake apology for not having change will usually keep them at bay. But there's just no nice way to say: *Sorry, my tits are worth more than twenty,* without sounding rude. Rudeness, well, that's a whole other problem.

I press the walk button and wait impatiently for the light to turn in my favor. A parade of buses and angry drivers speed down Mission Street with no regard for human life. The traffic and congestion are worse every year. College grads with dollar signs tattooed on their biceps flock to San Francisco with dreams of landing a job at the next big tech company. Some make it; some end up shooting heroin on the street.

Traffic slows to a stop and the crowd trudges forward. A woman carrying two Whole Foods bags walks straight at me with no intention of slowing down. The pedestrians are just as bad as the cars. I sidestep to give her a clear path; she moves past me without so much as a grateful glance. *Bitch.* I make it to the other side of the street and the mob disperses in all directions. Another group of men sits along the wall behind the west entrance to BART. I've always wondered why they have an entrance on both sides of the street. That's two holes in the ground. Two non-working escalators. Two walls. More assholes. One of the men leaves the wall and walks toward the sidewalk. A gang of pigeons takes flight in his wake. He pays no mind to the filthy birds circling his head. I get the feeling he's watching me. Timing my steps. He waits at the precise spot where our paths will cross, like two balls on a pool table. I consider breaking right to avoid him. Instead, I break my rule and look up. I haven't seen his face since I was four years old, but I know who he is, just like he knows who I am.

"Alee."

"Dad."

Truth be told, I've seen him before. Not like this. Not face-to-face. I've felt him watch me on more than one occasion as I walked home from school. Unlike the other creeps on the wall, his gaze never seemed dangerous. He's known who I am for a long time. I wonder why he's chosen today, of all days, to make himself known.

The only real memory I have of my father was the day he left. He stood in front of our house with a duffel bag slung over his shoulder, the way military men do when they head off to war. For years, I thought my father was a soldier. I pictured him crawling beneath barbed wire, sleeping in the rain, and yelling *sir, yes, sir!* Yes, I thought my father was Forest Gump.

To simply say I have abandonment issues is a massive understatement. I've craved attention from the opposite sex for as long as I can remember. In the first grade I had a male teacher. Even the smallest amount of praise from him made my heart soar. When Mom went to school for a parent-teacher conference and came home with a date, I felt like my prayers had been answered.

I awoke the morning after their first date to Mr. Jensen sitting at our dining room table with my father's old coffee mug and a satisfied grin. For a blissful three months, my mother seemed to be on board with Operation Make Mr. Jensen My Daddy. Until Mrs. Jensen showed up on our doorstep.

"How are you?" He takes a long drag on an almost finished cigarette. "You probably have to go. I'll let you get back to life."

The creator of my daddy-issues chose today of all days to crawl out from under his rock and speak to me. I'm not going to let him off that easy.

"Are you hungry?" Food is probably the only way I can keep him from running.

A slow smile spreads across his weathered face. "Food sounds good."

I take my father to Burger King. He places his order then pats his pockets like he's looking for his wallet or someone else's wallet.

"I got this." I fish my debit card out of my back pocket. I punch in the pin with my hand blocking the pad. It's a dick move, and I regret it instantly. When I look up, his head is turned away.

We don't speak as we wait for our food. I stand far enough away that people won't think we're together. He carries the tray to a table and attacks the meal like he hasn't had food in days. I'm not usually one to start a conversation. Apparently, neither is he. He seems nervous, ticky. He shrugs his shoulders a lot and looks around every few seconds. His eyes are everywhere all at once, yet he doesn't quite look at anything. Not directly. I fall into his line of sight again, then he returns to the tray. He picks up a crumb and places it in his mouth. Nothing is wasted with this guy. His leg bounces under the table, the way I do when I have to pee. Maybe he has to use the bathroom or maybe he's planning his escape. If I want answers, if I want to know who this man is and why he left, I need to ask him now.

"What should I call you?"

He smirks and shoves a fry in his mouth. "I guess it'd be too much to have you call me *Dad*."

"I've never used that word in reference to an actual person."

He looks shocked, happy.

"People call me Hawk." He eyes drift past me to the door like he's going to run. I'm not a runner. I'm a hider. If I were him, I would've stayed in the shadows. Unseen. Unknown. Now that he's in the open, he's a sitting duck. I'm locked and loaded with questions. He's not leaving here until I get some answers. I start big.

"Where have you been all these years?" I hide any trace of animosity in my tone and deliver the words as if they're for informational purposes like his absence had no personal effect on my life.

"Here and there," he says in between bites of his second Whopper.

The couple behind him wrinkle their noses and move to the other side of the restaurant. They probably think I'm a Bible thumper trying to save his soul with fast food. I'd rather be seen as a do-gooder than this homeless guy's daughter.

"Have you been on the street this whole time?"

He swallows a handful of fries then washes them down with a sip of coffee. His shoulders soften, and he leans back in the booth like we're two old friends shootin' the shit.

"I lived on a farm in Taft County for about three years, then I went to Portland." He shudders and takes another bite of his burger.

"Not a fan of Portland?"

"Portland was a bad idea." He crumples a napkin and uses it to wipe ketchup from the corner of his mouth. The guy probably hasn't changed his underwear in years, and he's wiping his mouth all proper and shit.

I'm an asshole.

"How do you make money?"

Generally, asking someone's profession isn't considered rude. Hawk's facial expression begs to differ. His dark brown eyes narrow as he contemplates his reply to my simple question.

"I worked on the farm," he says with a familiar coldness.

I try to imagine him in a pair of overalls, stacking hay with his big dirty hands and jet-black hair. He looks nothing like a farmer, or a bus driver, or any of the jobs my mother told me he had during their time together.

"I did a lot of other shit, too. All the bad shit addicts do for money." His eyes are emotionless like he's saying these things to hurt me. It doesn't work. Nothing hurts me. If there's one thing I inherited from this man, it's my skin. It isn't as weathered and damaged, but it's thick.

"Well, you must have been pretty damn good to last this long."

He regards me for a half a second, then breaks into a grin. He must steal Crest Whitestrips and use them every night because he's got the whitest teeth of any homeless drug addict I've ever seen.

"You grew into a beautiful woman." He looks as if he wants to say more but holds back. Anything more would be inappropriate. He might have provided a vital piece of my DNA, but he's still a stranger to me.

I try to return the compliment. "You seem healthy for a person in your situation."

He was twenty-six when I was born, that puts him at about forty-four. His black beanie and hoodie give off a young thug vibe. But his weathered complexion and wary eyes tell his real age. His fingers are covered in tattoos;

letters and numbers I'm too scared to read. I watch him eat and move and speak, looking for pieces of the man I remember. Through the grime, I see bits of him, of myself.

He lifts his coffee cup with a shaky hand. "I'm alive. That's good enough for me." Waking up in the morning must be a monumental achievement. He's survived another night on the street. Another high. Regular people don't think in those terms. We equate survival to tragedy. Surviving a car accident or a break-up, or worse, the death of someone you love.

"What about you? Have you had a good life?" He grips the paper coffee cup with two hands. It reminds me of the people from my old support group. I think most of them were only there for the free coffee. I stopped going after a month. A group of crybabies can't help me. Nothing helps.

"Depends on what you consider good," I say.

"A clean bed, food in your belly, and a pair of good shoes."

"Good shoes are a must," I agree.

"Oh, you have no idea, sweetheart."

We laugh lightheartedly for a few seconds, then return to silence.

"So, uh, what about your mom," he asks tentatively. "Is she…did she…"

"She's alive," I say. "And she's single."

He sets his coffee down. "So, she never remarried?"

"Did you?" I counter.

"No," he says with a bit of an attitude. "She was the love of my life. Once you have that kind of love, there's nothing after that."

Silence again.

I sip my soda and look around the restaurant. It's empty on our side; everyone is keeping a safe distance from my father. I know what they see when they look at this table. Someone dangerous, evil, a criminal. I look past the menacing exterior, the tattoos, the scars, and I see someone in pain. Self-inflicted and at the mercy of others. I see myself.

"I feel like I have so many things to ask, I don't know where to start." He shrugs. "What about school. Are you in college?"

"I'm a senior. If all goes well, I'll graduate next month. I don't' really know what I'm doing after that."

"You should go to college."

"Did you go to college?"

"I did," he smiles. "I got my bachelor's in English. I wanted to be a writer."

"Wow, I had no idea. Mom never told me those kinds of things about you. Nothing good."

His smile fades and he shrugs. "Nothing good to tell." He gathers the empty burger wrappers and places them on

10

the tray, then shoves a pile of napkins in the side pocket of his backpack. "Let's get out of here. I hate being cooped up."

We aren't in an elevator, we're in the dining room of a fast food joint. Hawk looks as if he's being tortured.

"I like being out in the open air. You know?"

I don't know. Nature isn't my thing. My bedroom is my sanctuary. "Yeah, let's go."

He holds open the door for me then he pulls a pack of Marlboro reds from his pocket. "Do you smoke?" He offers me a cigarette. So un-dad like.

"No."

"Good." He lights up, takes a long inhale. "Let's do this again. Eating, talking, whatever." I'm glad he suggested it because I wouldn't have. He puffs on his cigarette, blowing the smoke away from me. How considerate. "Oh, I know," he snaps his fingers. "Are you still friends with Frances's daughter? What was her name?"

"Bryn. And I don't want to talk about her." I start across the street to the corner where we just met.

"That doesn't sound good." He flicks his ash and swings his backpack onto his shoulder.

I think about what I've been through in the last week. I had a boyfriend, a best friend, and no father. Now I'm standing on the corner of 24th and Mission Street with Hawk.

"Was it a guy? It's always a fucking guy."

"Yeah, it was a guy."

Hawk tosses his cigarette butt into the gutter. "You want me to kick his ass?"

His offer makes me smile. A difficult feat. Hawk steps in front of me and clears the crowd. People go out of their way to avoid him. Hawk is probably going to get high the moment we part ways. He might never speak to me again but right now, watching him scare the shit out of the hipsters crossing Mission Street is comforting. I've had my father back for less than an hour and I already feel less alone.

SLUT.BITCH.WHORE.
Chapter Two

A FEW WEEKS AGO

Bryn is waiting for me at the end of the hall. The expression on her tan, round face tells me she knows.

Everyone knows. Bad news travels fast.

It wasn't like I was trying to hide it. I made Laine hold my hand as we walked down the street. He was hesitant, given our current status, but he didn't pull away, not even when we passed the donut shop where all the skaters hang out. That was less than twelve hours ago. I'll never underestimate a skater again. They might seem like they're only interested in riding a rail, but they're watching, just like the rest of us.

"Holy crap, Alee. What did you do?" Bryn whispers as I shove my books in our locker and take out her lip gloss. I apply a coat to my dry, adulterous lips in the little mirror hanging on the door and give her a who-cares shrug.

"So, everything they're saying is true?"

My eyes drop from the mirror as I focus on screwing the cap onto the tube. I want to sound defiant, unremorseful, but it comes out like a whimper. "Yes."

"Benny loves you, and you love him. Why would you bang his best friend?" She rests her chin on my shoulder and looks at me through the mirror. "Did Benny do something? Cause if he did, I'll kick his ass."

I love that she assumes I would never stoop this low unless I was provoked. I have nobody to blame. It was all me. I'd been thinking about sleeping with Laine since he got drunk and told me I was pretty. He wasn't flirting, just being nice. He's a good guy. I exploited the fact that he doesn't have a girlfriend. That he probably hasn't been laid in months or maybe ever.

The bell rings and Bryn hugs me. "I want to hear all the nasty details at lunch." She kisses my cheek then runs in the direction of her class. "And Alee," she yells from halfway down the crowded hall. "I still love you!" She sneers at the girls gawking my way then disappears around the corner.

There isn't a single moment of my life that I haven't shared with Bryn. We learned to ride the same bike, we wear the same size everything, and we even get our periods

14

on the same day every month. Bryn isn't just my best friend, she's the only real family I have.

The hall empties as the morning classes commence. Someone yells slut, the insult flies through the empty hall and lands at my feet in the form wet wadded up toilet paper.

I just can't today.

I slip past my homeroom, undetected by Mr. Sanders, and push open the door to the side yard. Nobody ever comes out here because this is where the dumpsters live. It's a small crevice between buildings that smells like rotten meat. It's my hiding place. I fit in perfectly among the trash. That's what I am now. I'm no longer the girlfriend of Benny Calderon. I'll be known as the bitch who broke his heart. Everyone loves Benny, including me. But loving Benny shouldn't define who I am. We started dating last fall, and at some point, I stopped being Alee Finch and became Benny's girlfriend. I've actually had people say, "Hi, Benny's girlfriend." They don't even ask my name like it doesn't matter. Like I don't matter.

Laine was my out. He always had a huge smile for me, bigger than Benny's sometimes. That's how I knew he would do it. Some smiles are friendly, and some are more. Figuring out which is which comes easy for me. Maybe it's a city thing. City kids learn to read people at a young age. Walking to the corner store and smiling at the wrong person could be the difference between an afternoon snack or being raped in a rat-infested alley.

I stay hidden among the dumpsters until the bell rings for lunch. I make a quick trip to the restroom to wash my hands before meeting Bryn. When I get to the cafeteria, I don't find my best friend waiting at the door. I spot her sitting at a table talking to Misty. I hate Misty. I hate all girls, except Bryn.

"Alee."

Over the last six months, I've listened to that voice say my name a thousand times. He's whispered it in my ear as I slept naked in his bed. He's yelled it from the football field and sung it in the shower. Of all the ways he's said my name, none have hurt the way it does now. My name falls off his tongue like the lash of a whip. Short, sharp, painful.

Heads and bodies turn in our direction when whispers of my arrival drift through the cafeteria. I don't want to do this with an audience. I push past him and zigzag through the crowd. People are yelling things as I pass. Mean things. *Slut. Whore. Bitch.* I fall through the side door, back to the serenity of my dumpsters. When I don't hear the door click closed behind me; I know I'm not alone.

"Alee," Benny says in between breaths. "I didn't know you could run that fast."

"There are a lot of things you don't know about me," I shoot back.

"Why are you doing this?" His voice quivers.

Oh no, don't be sad. Please don't be sad.

"Doing what?" I slap a smug look on my face and turn around.

He remains silent. Like he's waiting for me to morph into his version of me. The sweet, amiable girl I invented because I thought being with Benny Calderon was going to be this terrifically awesome experience. I thought Benny would make me happy. I was wrong.

His eyes search my face trying to catch a sliver of remorse. I give him nothing.

"What do you want, Benny?" I put my hands on my hips. "Do you want details? Do you want me to say I'm sorry?" Being mean feels good, powerful. My heart blackens with every hurtful word that escapes my lips. "Do you want to know if he was better than you?"

"No," he says through clenched teeth.

There it is. Anger. Come on, give it to me.

"Why Laine?" His voice cracks when he says his best friend's name.

The shame is heavy and smells like rotting vegetables. As hurtful as I want to be, I can't stand to see him in pain.

Anger, disgust—I get those emotions. I can live with being despised.

"Do you love him?"

"No," I say too quickly.

Benny exhales. He looks towards the sky in relief. I start to falter. This is what he does. He breaks me down with his charm. His words. His smile. And now his tears.

Benny wants a girlfriend who will wave at him from the stands and wear his jersey on game day. He wants a cheerleader. That was never me. I'm sick of trying to be something I'm not. I love Benny, but I don't want to sit on the sidelines. I want to matter. If I ace my American History test the same day he throws two interceptions, I expect him to congratulate me. Be happy *for* me. When Benny is sulking about an injury or a dropped pass, and I crack a joke or suggest we get ice cream, he looks at me like I'm a thoughtless bitch. He thinks my happiness is dependent on his success. If Benny fails, the world fails.

"How did it happen?" He doesn't really want to know the answer to this question. I can tell he wants me to reach for him, comfort him. Even though he'll probably push me away, he wants me to try.

"What did Laine say? Maybe the three of us should have this conversation together." As awkward as that would be, I don't want to be alone with Benny.

18

He clenches and releases his fists. "Laine didn't come to school."

I should've ditched too.

"Why Laine? You know he's like a brother to me." Benny shoves his hands in the pockets of his hoodie. Laine has the same one. They dress alike. They even kiss alike. But nothing about Laine is hard. He's kind and funny. He's a cheerleader too. We cheerleaders have to stick together.

"I saw him at Starbucks, and we decided to hang out."

Laine and I live a few blocks from each other in Noe Valley. I see him at Starbucks all the time. We usually just say hi, inquire about Benny, and then go our separate ways. Yesterday was the first time we ever had a real conversation. We talked for hours about movies and music; he even read *The Mission*—my favorite book of all time. It was nice to have a conversation about things that didn't involve sports or Benny.

"So how did you go from drinking lattes to fucking?" Benny's voice rises an octave.

I can't articulate it into words. It was a look that lasted too long. His hand brushing against mine when he placed his cup on the table. In the middle of a conversation about the latest episode of *Survivor*, Laine leaned his head towards me, and we kissed. Softy, quickly. He said he'd always wanted to kiss me.

19

"Alee." Benny steps towards me, and I snap back to reality. "Who made the first move?"

I stare at my dirty Chuck Taylors. Chucks are probably the only shoe you can wear dirty. The dirt makes them look vintage. Benny's white Jordans don't have a smudge on them. I want to step on his feet and ruin his flawless shoes. For every perfect Benny, there needs to be an equally fucked-up human. Someone dirty and ugly inside. That person is me.

"I did."

Benny nods in silent contemplation. "Okay, this is fixable. You screwed up; I get it. Since we're being honest. I did, too." He launches into a story about how he cheated on Halloween. I was in bed with the flu, and he was in bed with two cheerleaders from St. Ignatius High School. Catholic school sluts, is there anything worse?

"It feels so good to finally tell you." He has this look on his face like he's just done something amazing. Like telling me he cheated is a personal accomplishment. I'm not sure if I should pat him on the back or slap him across the face. He isn't even sorry; he looks almost proud. "Alee, come here." His tone is low, seductive.

Why is he making this so easy? I slept with his best friend. He cheated on me. We're toxic. I push him away. "Stop. I don't want your forgiveness."

"I don't care. I still forgive you." He steps closer, his silhouette blocking the sun. This is what he does. He keeps me in his shadow while he steals all the light. This isn't about me cheating anymore, it's about him forgiving me. I didn't ask for forgiveness and I don't want him.

"I want my own sun!" I yell and push him away.

He grabs my hand and yanks me back. "What are you saying?" He still doesn't get it. I have to be cruel. Ruthless.

I glare at him and smirk. He hates when I make this face. So, I do it. I make the bitch face and say, "Benny, this may come as a shock. But I don't *want* you." I pause to let the words sink in. "You're a good person, but you're a shitty boyfriend." I'm heavy on the attitude.

The light flickers out of Benny's eyes. He shudders and backs away like he's finally seeing me for the trash I am.

"The sun is big enough for everyone to share. You don't need to be the center of the universe. Once you learn that, you'll be the best boyfriend in the world, and I'll envy the girl who gets to love you." My voice cracks when I deliver the last line. The sudden burst of emotion surprises both of us. "Why are you doing this?" I plead as I try to prevent him from touching me. "Why do you want me, Benny?"

"I don't know." He steps towards me, and I'm back in his shade. "I love you." He loves me despite my intentionally hurting him. Betraying him. Maybe he sees something I

21

don't. Something worth saving. If he can see the good in me, if being with him makes me a better person, then Benny's shadow will be my home. I'll embrace my role. I'll cheer. He kisses me softly on the forehead. I've always loved that about him. A forehead kiss is the ultimate sign of affection. It can come from a lover, a friend, or a parent, but the meaning is always the same. Kissing someone on the forehead is a gesture of unconditional love.

"Why do you love me?" I release the tension in my arms and allow him to hold me. My lip twitches, begging for a smile. I don't have anything to smile about yet. Just the anticipation of what Benny is about to say. The checklist of good qualities he sees in me. Things the rest of the world is blind to. Things only my soulmate can see. Benny can have any girl in this school, and six months ago, he chose me. I need to know why.

"Where do I start?" He tilts his head to the side, the way he does when he's trying to be cute. "I love that you drink beer. That's huge for me."

Okay, not what I was expecting but not horrible.

"You don't complain when I'm late or forget to call. I like that a lot."

That wasn't romantic, but it's real. I appreciate real.

"And you look smoking hot in my jersey." He wraps his arms around my waist and tries to kiss me.

22

"No, keep going." There has to be more. Something legitimate he sees in me. Something more than beer and his jersey. Otherwise, what's the point?

"You want more?" He looks down at me with his famous crooked smile then rests his forehead against mine and exhales. The next thing out of his mouth will determine our fate. If he recites something even close to a speech in a Nicholas Sparks book, I'll stay.

Benny looks towards the sky and watches a flock of seagulls pass overhead. "You know, little bird"—he pauses as the birds switch formation and turn back the other way— "I love that I can drop by your house without calling, and you don't freak out about your hair or makeup. You consider a Diet Coke and a bag of Cheetos a meal. You never ask for more than I can give you. You're simple. It makes my life a lot easier."

He loves me because I eat Hot Cheetos?

Holy shit, I let myself get sucked back in. Benny doesn't love me, he doesn't even know what love is. "This isn't going to work." I try to move around him, he forces me to stay.

"You cheat on me with my best friend and you think I'm just going to let you walk away?"

"You don't own me, Benny." With all the strength I can muster, I push him away.

23

He steps to the side, blocking the only way out. I stare at the zipper on his hoodie, remembering the days my head rested over his heart and I felt save. Today is not one of those days. He steps closer, I flinch.

"You're a fucking bitch."

My instinct is to fight back. Tell him he's a cry baby and a terrible fuck. But I'm tired. Tired of Benny, tired of defending myself. I just want to leave. I want this part of my life to be over. I choose flight over fight. "Benny, please move. Let me go."

"You don't get to leave me, little bird. That isn't how this works." The sinister tone in his voice isn't new. I've heard him speak to me this way before. Only now the spell is broken. The alpha male role is played out. The dark look in his brown eyes is no longer sexy. Being owned isn't a turn on.

"Let me go." My voice is tired, but not weak. I look at the birds soaring overhead, the only witnesses to our breakup. I'd give anything to be one of them. Cageless and free. "I need to go."

"Why, so you can sneak behind my back and fuck more of my friends?" Benny laughs. It's an evil sound that sends a chill down my back. "You fucked my best friend, Alee." He tosses me and I stumble into the dumpster. "And I fucked yours."

BUCKET LISTS ARE BULLSHIT

Chapter Three

Most guys would've socked Laine in the face for breaking guy code, but Benny made sure the school knew I wasn't worth it. As far as the world is concerned, Benny never loved me. I'm just some slut he passed around to his friends. *Friends.* Such a bullshit word. I haven't seen or spoken to my so-called best friend since I left Benny by the dumpsters. I need to process what he said about Bryn. I process best in solitude.

Solitude and Netflix.

In between binge-watching *Orange is the New Black*, I researched online schools. Mom seemed open to the idea until she saw the price tag. Online education isn't cheap. If she were drinking, it'd be easy. I'd take her credit card and pay for it like I do everything else when she's on a bender. She's been sober eight months. That might seem like something to celebrate, but I know better.

The house phone rings and Mom yells for me to answer it. I roll off the sofa and walk through the dining room to the kitchen. Our house is a typical San Francisco tract home— hardwood floors, high ceilings, mold.

I check the caller ID. It's Bryn. She couldn't get through on my cell so she went old school and called the landline. I threw my cell phone into Lake Merced. Even though I erased all our texts, just looking at that thing reminded me of the nights I fell asleep with it next to my pillow. The tinkling sound sent my heart into spasms. His calls, his texts, his kisses consumed my world. I've seen what a love like that can do, and I want no part of it.

I still catch Mom sitting at the window with a drink in one hand and her wedding photo in the other. She sits and waits, hoping my father will come walking around the corner. Come back to her.

"Hi, Bryn."

"Oh em gee, Alee. Where have you been? So much has happened." It's clear by her rambling that she hasn't spoken to Benny or she's just pretending things are normal. That she didn't fuck my boyfriend.

"This call is costing you minutes, just come over."

"You're worth my minutes, boo."

She's trying really hard. Too hard.

Thirty minutes later she's at the door. Mom is home, so we go straight to my room. I haven't spoken to Bryn since the morning I broke up with Benny. We aren't the kind of friends who need to check in every day. She's on the dance team, the swim team, and she plays soccer. Unlike Benny, Bryn doesn't need a gang of people cheering her on. She does it for personal satisfaction, not popularity.

I close my bedroom door and grab my iPod from the dresser. I scroll to a random song and hit play. The mood doesn't call for music, but it will make it harder for Mom to eavesdrop. Bryn doesn't kick off her shoes and lay across my bed like she normally does. She stands with her back against the door, ready to bolt.

"So, what happened?" she finally asks. "Why did Benny break up with you?"

"First of all, I dumped him."

"Of course," Bryn agrees like I'm asking her to choose a side. She should be on my side no matter what. Deep down I know Benny is telling the truth about him and Bryn. He's a lot of things, a liar isn't one of them.

I tell her I loved Benny, but he wasn't *the one*. I tell her he was a sunshine stealer and a crybaby. She asks if I like Laine.

"No, he was just a means to an end. Have you seen Laine? Is he okay?"

"He's doing fine," Bryn assures me. "I know like six girls who are dying to go to prom with him. Like they will kill to be his date."

Something brews in my chest. Jealousy, maybe. Not because girls want to kill for Laine, I envy him because his life is back to normal—better than normal. The wrath I've endured since Benny and I broke up is so much worse than I anticipated. Benny was never going to be the love of my life. I was hoping to slip back into oblivion once we were no longer a couple. All those jerks who didn't bother to ask my name when Benny and I were together, know it now. Just the mention of Alee Finch will initiate relentless gossip. Stories about Laine and me. Me and the wrestling team. Me and the vice-principal, have flooded social media.

"I still don't get why you did it. Why would you cheat on someone like Benny?"

Clearly, Bryn has no idea about Benny's confession. Part of me doesn't even want to bring it up. I don't want any more Benny-related drama. I pick at the fuzz on my comforter and form them into a ball. "Benny is a cheese pizza. I want a supreme with extra meat and cheese in the crust. I want every bite to be new and magical. Not the same boring flavor over and over again." I toss the ball of fuzz at her. She watches it float to the floor near her feet and doesn't laugh at my pizza analogy. She looks at me like I'm crazy, or worse, a bad person. "I could die tomorrow." I cringe at my choice of words.

"Alee, no."

I shake my head. "It's not that." I haven't had those thoughts in a long time. It's an unspoken, somewhat forgotten day that no longer exists. "I'm seventeen, and I've only been in love once. I could die, he could die, we all could. An epic earthquake could wipe us out at any minute. I don't want to leave this earth having loved only one person in my life."

"Why didn't you break up with him before you slept with Laine?"

"Benny wouldn't let me."

Bryn rolls her eyes. Bryn only rolls her eyes when she's arguing. *Are we arguing?*

"All you had to do was tell him you didn't want to be with him anymore," she says as if she's defending him.

Whose side is she on?

"I was a thing he possessed. He wouldn't let me walk away. Hell, Bryn, he was ready to forgive me." I think about the look on his face when he tried to pull me into his arms. "Benny hates losing. He got cheated on. I know he sees that as a fail."

"But he cheated on you." Bryn looks at her feet. I know her. She's remorseful, scared. Bryn has a pattern of liking the same boys I do. I chalk it up to our being best friends. We have the same taste in food and music. Swooning over the same boy in fifth grade isn't the same. I loved Benny. He was my first everything.

She remains glued to my door, waiting to see if I'm going to punch her in the face. I tap my mattress, and she moves from the door to sit beside me. I'm not mad at her for sleeping with Benny. There is nothing Bryn could ever do to make me hate her. She's got a killer body, her hair is always perfectly messy, and she can burp the alphabet—all qualities I would totally hate in any other human. She is my only friend. I need Bryn in my life. Without her, I'm alone.

"It's true, then?" The question is rhetorical.

"It wasn't even that great. You made it seem like he was so great." She's playing this off like she just stole a pair of old jeans from a pile going to Goodwill.

"I had no frame of reference. That's why I slept with Laine. Now I know Benny was just meh."

Bryn kicks off her shoes. "Less than meh. He was eh."

"Definitely, eh."

We compare notes on Benny, and she catches me up on school gossip like today is just a regular Tuesday. At five-thirty the alarm on Bryn's phone goes off.

"I gotta go. I have swim practice at seven." She zips up her hoodie and gathers her shoes from under the bed. She's wearing black high-top Nikes with a bright pink swoosh. I should hate them, but I don't. They're so Bryn. "I'm meeting my new coach today." She smiles up at me as she ties her shoes. "They think I'm Olympic material." She bites her lower lip and gives me a please-don't-hate me look.

"You promised to suck at one thing this year."

"I tried to suck, but I can't help it. I'm awesome."

I open my door, and she walks out in front of me then stops.

"Wait, I have an idea." She pulls our bucket list off the wall. It began as a joke. We listed goofy things like run a marathon and kiss ten boys before we turned twenty-one. Then Bryn started getting serious about life. She added: be nominated for a Nobel Peace Prize, win an Olympic medal, attempt the swim from Alcatraz. While I added superficial things like find out who killed Tupac and get a boob job. Bryn scribbles something on the list, then sticks it back on the wall.

#11 – ~~Sleep with your best friend's boyfriend.~~

"Adding it to our bucket list makes me look less like a dick," she says as she walks out of my room.

I look at the only thing crossed off our list. Now it feels more like an accomplishment and less like a stab in the back.

As I walk Bryn to the door, she stops to say goodbye to Mom. My mother had a falling out with Bryn's parents over my father. When he left, mom accused them of hiding him or something. I'm not clear on the details; I just know they don't speak. Ever. But she's polite to Bryn.

"See you later, Mrs. Finch."

"Can you stay for dinner? It's nearly finished." Mom pulls a covered casserole dish from the wall oven.

"She has to go." I push Bryn forward. "I'm walking her to the bus stop. I'll be right back."

Bryn lives in Bernal Heights, near Benny. Did they meet at one of the hipster cafés on Cortland Avenue? Did she sneak into his father's man cave after Benny's parents were asleep, the same way I did when we first started going out? If I truly loved Benny, maybe I'd be hurt by Bryn's actions. Thankfully, Benny Calderon is irrelevant to me. I won't allow him to take up space in my head or my heart. We graduate in a month, and Benny will be off at his fancy college and out of my life forever.

Three people are waiting for the bus when we get to the corner. This line runs every six minutes, so you never have to wait long for the bus.

"I do suck at one thing," Bryn says as we join the others at the bus stop. "I suck at being your friend." I look at her to see if she's joking. She's not. "I never should've had sex with Benny."

She loops her arm around mine and rests her head on my shoulder. She's two inches taller than me, so it looks really weird. We catch the attention of a man in a black suit. Tall, dark, sort of handsome.

"You can fuck whoever you want," I tell her, and the black-suit guy raises an eyebrow. He's cute for an old dude. "I slept with his best friend, and he slept with mine. We're even."

Bryn straightens up. "Oh my God. I never looked at it like that."

The bus pulls to a stop, and the customary line forms at the front door. Bryn boards the bus, stopping to wave midway to the back. I blow her a kiss. I'm sure Benny made it seem like she was the most important thing in the world to him. She might have been for fifteen minutes of foreplay and six minutes of sex. Okay, maybe seven. Benny has a way of making you feel special just because you're in his presence. That's the problem. He will always be more important than you. It makes his love seem like charity.

"Excuse me." The black-suit man is standing behind me.

"Sorry, I'm not getting on." I sidestep out of his way.

"Did I hear you say your best friend slept with your boyfriend?"

33

"Ex."

"Yes?"

"No."

"No, she didn't sleep with him?"

"Yes, she slept with him. But he is my ex." *Now.*

"Wow, that's pretty fucked up." He places his hand in the pocket of his pants to pull out his bus pass. "You must be a really understanding friend if you can forgive her for that." He steps onto the bus.

Nosy bastard.

I watch him walk to the back and sit down, eight rows away from Bryn. As the bus pulls away, he smiles at me. I flip him off.

BABY CARROTS
Chapter Four

I found out Bryn was dead from the guy at the corner store. I walked to the counter to pay for a can of Sprite and a Twix, and he said, "Hey, isn't that your friend?" He pointed to the TV hanging on the wall behind him. He usually had on a soccer game or a foreign news channel. That day it displayed the building where Bryn had swim practice. Her picture, along with her new coach's, sat side by side in little boxes, the word *victims* written beneath their names in bold white letters.

The man who shot Bryn didn't know her. He was in the building to kill his wife and Bryn's swim coach. He purchased a handgun, waited two weeks for the background check, and legally obtained his weapon. He killed his wife, wounded her lover, and murdered my best friend. Three other people were injured, some by gunfire, mostly from the fight to get the gun away from the angry husband. He was a big guy who also had a large hunting knife with him. During his confession, he told the detectives he wanted to chop his wife up and shove the pieces down her lover's throat.

If Bryn hadn't clocked a record-breaking time at a regional swim meet, the scout wouldn't have seen her and invited that coach here to train her. The scout and the coach started having an affair that ended in the most devastating shooting of the year. Bleeding to death in a puddle of chlorinated water was not Bryn's destiny. We live in a world where someone's life is at the mercy of an angry man's ego.

I ran home and found my mother had already drowned herself in a bottle of bourbon. She met me at the door and sobbed on my shoulder. I didn't shed a single tear in front of her. She didn't deserve my tears; I wouldn't acknowledge hers. She was drunk on the day I needed her most.

Bryn's mom, Frances, called early the next morning and asked me to come over and help her pick out an outfit to bury their daughter in. That night I slept in Bryn's bed wearing her dirty pajamas. Her mother slept at the end of the bed. The next day we went through all of Bryn's clothes, nothing felt right. We settled on a dress she wore to a cousin's wedding last summer. It's blue, our favorite color. Frances asked me if I want any of the Bryn's clothes. Bryn is tall, was tall, with a swimmer body. I'm average height with hips that look like I never say no to dessert.

Bryn's parents cling to me like I'm the last part of her. Like I will disappear, and they'll have nothing, like me. Without her I am nothing.

Four days pass in a blur of tears and casseroles. Leaving Bryn's house is like being spit out of a wormhole into another dimension. Inside Bryn's flat, she's still alive. She's in the walls, the furniture, the air. She will always live in that space. Out here, where the air is clean, and the sky is blue, she no longer exists. It's only nine in the morning, and it's already warm. Bryn hated hot days. She loved the fog. The sun shines its fucking rays on the sidewalk in front of me with no regard for my feelings. The sun doesn't care Bryn is dead.

I walk to the bus stop and catch the 24-line. I see Bryn in everything. Her wavy brown hair on a lady riding a bike. Her smile on the face of a little girl running towards Day Street Park. I get off the bus and walk to Starbucks. I order a Chai Tea Latte, Bryn's drink. I sip it as I walk to my house—the only place on earth that doesn't remind me of Bryn. My house is another world altogether.

I find Mom sitting in her robe at the dining room table, sipping something from a coffee mug. I don't say hi. Neither does she. I take a shower and search my closet for the black dress I wore to a dance our freshman year. Bryn was asked to go by a boy in her science class. She begged me to tag along in case he turned out to be a jerk. He did. She ditched him, and we spent the evening eating cookies and talking shit about our classmates.

I find the dress hanging behind a winter coat my mother bought me two years ago. It's a bright pink puffy thing that I wouldn't be caught dead wearing. The woman knows nothing about me. I yank the coat off its hanger and stomp on it, then kick it into the back of the closet. I pull the dress over my head, and it settles over my body. The dress is black with triangle cut-outs around the waist that flares slightly at the bottom. It's not too girly, not too fancy, not too anything. I dig out the black tights I wore with the dress from the back of my sock drawer. I put on a little makeup and a dab of perfume, the one Bryn gave me for Christmas. It's a tester she stole from Macy's at Union Square. We don't even know what kind it is because the bottle just says "Tester." I grab my black-and-white Chucks from the floor and a navy blue hoodie from the hook on the back of my chair. I don't think hoodies are proper funeral attire, but it's cold, and it's all I have.

Our bucket list catches my eye. The dark black line Bryn drew through the last entry makes me smile. I should cry at all the things she didn't get to do. The medals she'll never earn, the goals she'll never meet. I don't look at the list and vow to accomplish these things in her honor. I look at the list and realize they were never going to happen. Maybe I should thank Benny. If it weren't for him, Bryn wouldn't have crossed a single thing off our list.

I walk into the living room and sit on the sofa to put on my shoes. Mom is still in her robe gripping the mug with both hands. I bet she isn't even drinking coffee.

"You're not going to the funeral?" I ask to make it official.

She shakes her head.

"Can't you put the bullshit aside for one day?"

"It isn't that simple." She sighs. "Frances said some pretty awful things to me when your dad left. I just can't…"

"This isn't about you!" I scream. "This isn't about Frances or my father—it isn't even about Bryn. It's about me! You never think of me!" My throat burns from the amount of force my words use to fly from my chest. "You are so fucking selfish!" I slam the front door. The windows rattle and tears slide down my cheeks.

I ride in the limo with Bryn's parents and sit beside them during the church service. The weight of their grief is almost unbearable. I don't cry. I can't. I'm the only thing holding them together. Holding them for Bryn.

A lot of people attend the service at Saint Kevin's. I hear someone say it's close to three hundred. Less than half drive out to the cemetery. It's mostly just family and close friends.

I recognize some of her cousins from the birthday parties and holidays I spent with Bryn's family. I was her tag-along. The friend with no family. *What am I now? Who am I without her?*

We line up as Bryn's coffin is lowered into the ground. Someone hands me a flower, and I toss it into the hole. It doesn't feel like goodbye. Nothing about today seems real. Nobody speaks in the limo. It's the most peaceful silence I've experienced in a long time. I wonder if Bryn is in another realm watching us. We talked about other dimensions once. Heaven and Hell. She didn't believe in any of it. Bryn thought death was nothingness. I refuse to believe she no longer exists. Bryn will always be alive in some reality, some other world, to me.

We return to St. Kevin's for the reception. Bryn's parents are absorbed into the crowd. People offer kind words and long hugs. Her parents nod and smile, but they don't hear a damn thing these people are saying. You can't console those who don't want consolation. Nothing you can say, or cook, will bring their daughter back. I swim in the hurt and pain with them. Sometimes pain is the only emotion that makes sense. When you're hurting this badly, pain is the only thing that keeps you tethered to reality.

I meet four girls from her dance team claiming to be her best friend. That's the kind of person she was. I'm sure Bryn made each of them feel like they were special. But I was her soulmate.

People keep asking about my mom. I say she had to work. After the sixth or seventh lie, I look for someplace to hide. I spot an empty seat in the far corner of the hall and make my way across the room. The tights I'm wearing don't fit. I just realize that now. I sit and watch people drift into the room. Some smile, I want to scream at them, tell them smiling isn't allowed. Through the crowd I see Laine. He's wearing a suit, and he wears it very well. He stops to shake hands and hug various adults. I can tell from the warm look on their faces, they think Laine is a good boy. I know better. He makes his way to me and I pretend my heart doesn't beat harder the closer he gets.

"Hi." I stand to greet him.

He pulls me into his arms. "I'm sorry, Alee." Laine feels good, so good that I start to feel warmth again.

"Thanks." I have no clue why I'm thanking him. Perhaps for his sympathy, his presence, his arms. I pull my wall back into place and ignore the smell of his cologne lingering in my hair. The top of my tights rolls over my belly, I pinch the side of my dress to snap them back into place.

"Is Benny here?" I'm just inquiring to make sure his face doesn't pop up next.

"No. Finals."

"Oh yeah. School is the last thing on my mind."

"Have you heard back from any colleges? I can't remember if you ever told me where you applied."

"Funny."

"Why is that funny?"

"My perfect C-average isn't going to get me into beauty school let alone college. I'm thinking maybe a career in fast food. What about you?"

"I see hard labor in my future."

"You win."

"I didn't realize we were playing a game."

"We are. It's called life."

Laine hands me a flask. "We're totally crushing it."

I laugh because his statement is the furthest thing from the truth. The only difference between me and Bryn is that everyone knows she's dead. I'm dead on the inside, where no one can see. I hand the flask back without taking a sip.

"I got into UC Davis." Laine loosens his tie. But I don't have the kind of parents who saved for college."

"Like Benny's parents."

"Exactly."

Benny is such a fucking yuppie.

"Yeah, he kind of is." Laine laughs.

"Did I say that out loud?"

"You did." Laine smiles. "You're a trip; you know that?"

42

"You're white trash, and I'm a loser. I don't know what Benny's over-achieving ass ever saw in us."

"Hey, speak for yourself. I'm Irish and Italian."

I roll my eyes. "That's what all white guys say."

Being alone with Laine gives me feels. I don't want to feel those feels. I want to live in the pain a little longer. I owe it to Bryn. I politely walk away from Laine to the other side of the room, the side with food. Laine follows me the same way he followed me that night.

Funeral food is like every other party food. Pinwheel sandwiches, mini-meatballs in a brown sauce, wilted salad, and an assortment of cheese and crackers. Laine plucks a cucumber from the tray. He dips it in ranch then shoves it in his mouth with an inappropriately timed sexy smile.

"Bryn hates baby carrots. She said there was something unnatural about them."

"Toss them." Laine points to the trash receptacle. "She's right, they look like fat little baby fingers." He inspects a dried out digit shaped carrot.

I pick up the tray and carry it to the trash. "This is for Bryn." The carrots make a raucous as they spill into the bin. A few people glance my way, not for long. Too much eye contact and they'll have to acknowledge me, speak me, console me.

Laine tosses his carrot in from a few feet away. "Bryn for the win." He holds pose a few seconds the way Steph Curry does when he hits a three.

We return to the buffet where Frances is speaking to Bryn's English teacher. She was an honor student so we never had classes together.

"Bryn was smart," I tell Laine because he's the only one here who will listen. "She had a 4.0 for, like, ever."

I remember watching her study, wondering where all that information went. She was like a sponge, absorbing everything around her. Bryn immersed herself in life. She was always moving, always busy with practice of some kind, volunteering, studying, me. I was a project too. She tried like hell to get me involved, get me out of my shell. My spirit animal is a crab; shells are my thing.

Laine and I move to the stage on the other side of the room. A bunch of unattended kids run back and forth squealing like baby pigs. Laine knows a couple of them. They jump on him as soon as he sits down and beg for piggyback rides. He obliges. Laine is a nice guy. I like Laine. That's probably why I fucked him.

"Are any of these yours?" It's a joke, but you never know. "That one kind of has your eyes." I point to the little girl clinging to his back. He gently lets her down and she runs off.

"I volunteer at an after-school program at the rec. At first, it was just something to add to my college applications, but I liked it so I stayed."

"You really are a good guy, aren't you?"

"You say that like it's a bad thing."

"I owe you an apology, for that day. For sucking you into my shit show. You didn't deserve that."

His shoulder leans into mine. "No apology necessary. Honestly, I could tell you and Benny weren't gonna make it." Laine is Benny's best friend, he knows all about Benny's side chicks. Maybe that's why he did it. I wonder if Bryn knew it too.

A parent finally comes to discipline the kids and coerces them off the stage with the promise of cupcakes. We're finally alone.

"I missed you, you know, after." Laine looks at me cautiously. This isn't exactly the most appropriate place to have this conversation. "We had some good times. All of us, I mean."

I can only recall one time when me, Benny, Laine, and Bryn hung out. We took the L-Train to the beach. Bryn saw some of her soccer buddies and ended up ditching me. I don't think Laine and Bryn said ten words to each other. Benny, on the hand, couldn't keep his mouth shut. He babbled and flirted with Bryn the entire train ride. I didn't see it as flirting back then. Maybe subconsciously. That's why I didn't care when Bryn ditched me for her *other* friends. It's why I stopped inviting Bryn to hang out when Benny was around. I never asked Bryn when she slept with Benny or how many times. It didn't matter. Benny and I weren't meant to be, no matter how hard we tried to convince ourselves otherwise. First love is like the chickenpox: you get it once and then you never get it again. That kind of love, that obsessive, blind love will ruin you.

"I think it's safe to talk about it now without having to pretend we're sorry. I'm not sorry."

Laine breaks into another sexy smile, one that would make a normal girl blush. "I do feel bad, though. Benny is my best friend."

"Yeah, you look really torn up about it."

"I felt bad for you. The way people treated you." He takes my hand and rubs his thumb along my knuckles. "But I never regretted it."

I look from my hand to his face. His sweet, sexy, manly face. Laine looks more like an adult than Benny. Benny can't even grow a goatee. Laine has stubble at two o'clock in the afternoon.

"I wouldn't have forced you to do it if I was going to regret it later."

"Forced me? I don't remember it like that."

"You have to admit it was my idea."

"The second you took my hand, I knew we were gonna bang." He tries to play it off like it was something casual. Sharing a sexual experience is always personal; who we were when it happened made every touch, every kiss, so much more.

Nobody in this room cares that Laine and I are speaking. Not a single person is looking our way. It proves how insignificant high school is. Sleeping with Laine, breaking up with Benny, none of that matters. Nothing we did would have stopped this day from happening.

"I don't even know why I chose you," I lie. "I could've used so many other guys to get back at Benny."

"If it had been someone else, it would've broken him," Laine says with absolute certainty. He is right. I didn't want to break Benny; I just wanted out. How could Laine possibly know that unless he wanted out too.

When the speeches start, Bryn's parents ask me to say something, but I refuse. I have no words. After Bryn's soccer coach speaks, a politician takes the stage and begins to preach about gun control. I head for the door. Laine meets me there with my hoodie, and we walk to the bus stop. The afternoon fog has settled in for the night. I zip my hoodie to my neck but I can't do anything about the icy breeze flowing up my dress.

"You don't have a car?" he asks.

"I don't have a license."

"I have mine but my dad won't pay for my insurance, so until I get a job, I'm stuck with this." He holds up his bus pass. Being with Laine makes me feel like less of a loser.

Benny constantly teased me about taking the bus. Once he got his car, public transportation was beneath him. It's easy to confuse arrogance for confidence when you're wearing first-love blinders. Now I see Benny Calderon in all his stuck-up glory. I understand why Laine is his best friend—balance. Every douchebag needs a good guy around to vouch for him.

Me and Laine jump on the 24-line bus and go back to Noe Valley. We sit next to one another, but neither of us speaks the entire ride. I pull the string to alert the driver I want off at the next stop. The bus pulls to the curb, and we exit through the back door.

"Thanks for today. If you hadn't been there, I'd probably…" I can't finish my thought because I don't want to imagine a scenario that doesn't include Laine's sweet face and warm hands. He saved me today, not just from the crowd and the questions, but from myself.

I didn't expect to see Benny at the funeral, but I wouldn't have been surprised either. He did sleep with her. A lot of kids from school peppered the crowd. Kids who didn't know her. Teachers who never taught her. Benny has been inside of Bryn and he's too busy to make an appearance.

Laine gives me a hug. He's warm against the cold June gloom. "See you at graduation." He kisses my forehead. "Call me if you want to hang out, talk, whatever."

Whatever with Laine sounds nice. Which is why I vow never to see him again.

FOR THE BIRDS

Chapter Five

NOW

Loneliness makes you do crazy things. I find myself making up reasons to walk by the BART station where Hawk hangs out. I've cruised the area five or six times since the day he spoke to me. The day after Bryn's funeral. Had she been alive or if I hadn't dumped Benny, I probably wouldn't have acknowledged Hawk. I would've kept walking, pretended I was someone else. The person I was before I lost Bryn or the girl Benny wanted me to be. The universe has a strange way of bringing people together and tearing them apart. The universe is mother fucker.

My stalking finally pays off and I catch Hawk at the spot. Half a dozen men sit on the concrete wall panhandling and scaring tourist. Hawk greets me with a warm smile and a gentle pat on the back. We aren't at the hugging stage yet.

He introduces me to some of his friends. He classifies them into two groups: good dudes and motherfuckers I should never encounter alone. Even though we've just met, these people tell me their life stories, like they need me to know what led them to the street. Some are difficult to hear. Tales of unimaginable abuse, hopeless addiction, and old-fashioned bad luck. I find things in common with every single person I meet. Most of them are looking for a light at the end of the tunnel. A way off the streets, a better life.

Not my dad.

He walked away from his job, his home, his child—to sleep in the rain and shit in a bucket. We're in San Francisco, one of the richest cities in the world, and my father eats food from a trash can. Not because he has to. Bryn's family owns an apartment building with a convenience store on the bottom floor. Bryn's father, Ray, would've done everything in his power to help his best friend. When Hawk left, Mom was convinced Ray was letting him stay in one of their empty apartments. Ray swore he hadn't seen him and was not giving him money. Mom never believed him. She's let that belief eat at her for nearly fifteen years. If Hawk showed up on Ray's doorstep right now, I bet he'd take him in, now more than ever. There are people in this world who care about Hawk, and all he cares about is his next high. He didn't just leave me, he left us all.

We sit on the wall behind BART sharing a bag of BBQ chips—his favorite. I know this because Mom never allows me to buy them. There's a long list of banned items that remind Mom of my father. BBQ chips, Red Stripes, Marvin Gaye, sunny days.

"How's school?" Hawk asks trivial questions, things a father would ask at dinner. "Are you getting good grades."

"I do all right." I lie like a good teenager.

"I saw some kids in caps and gowns last night. Are you graduating soon?"

Our graduation was two days ago. I didn't bother telling Mom. I wasn't walking in it anyway. Even if I had, no one would have been there to clap for me. I've always been annoyed by those families, the ones who show up for life events and clap the loudest. Like clapping is a sign of their love. The louder they clap, the more they love their child. What does it say for the kids who don't have anyone there to clap for them? Yeah. Exactly.

Mom doesn't care that she missed my graduation; she never even asked if I was graduating. In this parallel universe, Hawk did.

"I have to go to summer school so I'll get my diploma in the mail." I toss a handful of chips to the pigeons. It causes a frenzy.

"Hey, man." Hawk snatches the bag. "Don't waste food on those fuckers." People turn at the rise of his voice.

"Sorry." I wipe my hands on my jeans.

One of his friends, the one with no front teeth, makes a gesture for him to chill out.

"No, I'm sorry." He hands the bag back. "I had a bad experience with pigeons once."

There's a story there, one I'd love to hear but I have a feeling Hawk doesn't want to relive it.

"I'm done. You can have the rest." I fold the open side in half and place the bag on the wall between us. "Or your friend can have them." I wave to the toothless guy.

He waves back.

"No, Paul is gluten-free."

Only in San Francisco.

I LIKE CAKE
Chapter Six

Here's the thing about living in the city: you run into the same people all the time even when you go out of your way to avoid them. I'm planted in the corner of the tea shop devouring a slice of cheesecake when Laine walks in. Apparently, I'm avoiding Starbucks for nothing. He orders a drink then walks right over to me.

"Since when do you drink tea?"

"So you are avoiding me." He sets his mug on the table and sits in the chair across from me.

"I'm not avoiding you."

"I saw you leaving Cala Foods on Tuesday. I called your name and you literally ran from me."

"You saw that?"

"It's kind of hard to miss a girl sprinting down Noe Street carrying a gallon of milk in one hand and a twenty-four pack of toilet paper in the other."

"When you gotta go…" Insinuating I had to take a monster shit in front of a boy should make me want to puke. Laine isn't that kind of boy. Though, today especially, he doesn't look boyish. "Why are you all dressed up?"

"I had a job interview."

"That's very grown-up. Where?"

"My dad works for the city. He scored me an interview with his department. The waitlist is a mile long, but fingers crossed."

I cross my fingers for him.

"What about you?"

"I'm officially a high school graduate." I pull a folded envelope from Bryn's tote bag and hand it to Laine. He opens it and removes my crumpled diploma. He makes a disapproving face at my treatment of the document I've worked four years to earn. "What? It's just a piece of paper."

"I guess." Laine sets it on the table. "Doesn't your mom want to frame it or something?"

"I don't have that kind of mom." I fork my cheesecake. "Since you're crashing my graduation party, here." I offer him a bite.

Something sad fills Laine's eyes. He accepts the cheesecake and washes it down with his tea. "We can do better than this." He points to my plate. "Let's get out here."

55

Laine leaves his tea and we head outside. His hands are in the pockets of his dress pants. He looks like a stockbroker or a law student. He looks hot. I look around for an excuse to run. No stray dogs or bees in sight.

"I spent the last of my money on that cheesecake, so unless you received a signing bonus, I think this is where we call it a day."

"My mom made lasagna last night and my old man won't miss a few beers." The idea feels innocent. It might be on Laine's part. I was the school slut and sluts can't be trusted.

"I don't know. I told Bryn's parents I would stay over." I spend a few nights a week at their place. It makes them feel less alone.

"Really? That's how you want to spend your Friday night? Watching the Hallmark channel?" I laugh at his accuracy. "Come on, Alee. My parents are working all night. Help me break some rules for once."

When he puts it that way, how can I say no?

Laine's house smells like garlic and onions. It smells like a place where a family eats dinner together and speaks to one another more than once a week.

Our footsteps echo through the long empty hall that runs the length of the house. Midway down is the kitchen. Laine stops in for a bottle of water, then we go to his room at the end of the hall. I pause at the door while Laine plugs his iPod into the speaker on his desk then hangs his suit jacket in the closet.

"Can you crack open the window." He walks into the bathroom and turns on the faucet.

Laine's room is so large, his bed sits in the middle of the room, you can access it from either side. One side of my bed butts up against the wall, and I don't even have a headboard. It isn't like Mom doesn't make money, she does—good money. She doesn't feel the need to better our lives.

The windows are large and covered with blue and gray checked curtains, the kind on display at IKEA. I flip the lock on the window and slide it open, the smell of fog and city flows into the room. I've only been in Benny's room a few times. His mother wouldn't allow us to be alone in the house. I spent most of my time in their family room. Laine was the first guy I banged in an actual bed. I never took Benny to my house. I gave zero fucks if my mom caught us having sex. My biggest fear was Benny seeing my mother wasted off her ass and making a fool out of me.

I slide out of my Chucks and pull my hoodie off. "It's cool you have your own bathroom," I say to fill the silence. "We only have one bathroom, it's just me and mom but it sucks to share. How did you swing the good room?"

Your parents must really love you.

"They do."

I turn and find Laine watching me. "Did I say that out loud?"

"You did." He plops onto his bed and leans back on his elbows like I'm about to put on a show for him.

"The last time I was here…"

"It was awkward," he finishes my thought.

I walk to the bed and pull him up by his tie. I stop short of kissing him. I look into his eyes, those sweet eyes. "Are we friends?"

"Yes." Laine caresses my face. "For now."

I release his tie and move back to the window where the cold breeze is finally doing its job. "I was never friends with Benny. In fact, I sort of hated him. If I do this again—fall for a guy—I want it to be with someone I like."

"I've always liked you. Back before you and Benny, we were friends. No matter what happens between us now, I'll always be there for you."

"You can't make that kind of declaration. Who knows where we'll be two years from now. Who we'll be. You could turn into a douche."

"Not gonna happen." Laine unties his dress shoes. "Even if I do, you can't be friends with a douche?" He slips his shoes off then starts unbuttoning his shirt.

"Why are you undressing?"

58

He removes the white collared shirt and places it on the back of his desk chair. "I don't want to wrinkle my good clothes."

"Should I leave?" I take a step towards the door. His parents are gone for the night, we don't have to hide out in his room. We have the entire house to ourselves, and somewhere in here is a perfectly good lasagna.

"If this is making you uncomfortable you can leave." He unzips his pants and lets them fall to the floor. "Or you can stay." He is pretending to be sexy, as if that were possible.

Laine stands confidently in the center of his room wearing a white t-shirt and black boxer briefs. You couldn't pay me stand that naked in front of anyone. Not even myself. There's a reason I don't have a full length mirror in my room.

"I guess I'll stay." I shrug and lean against the desk.

"There are some people in this world you are meant to know. Whether you become friends or lovers or even enemies, sometimes people are your destiny. Alee Finch, I think you are mine."

I've never been someone's destiny. It's a lot of pressure. What if I don't live up to his fantasy? What if I allow myself to fall in love with him and he realizes later that he was wrong? What if I walk away and he was right?

I consider his grandiose statement as I look around the room. The posters of sports teams, a pennant from UC Davis, a small framed picture of his parents on the table beside his bed tell me Laine is a good guy. I've never heard stories about him at school. No scorned ex-girlfriends. No pregnancy scares. In fact, I'd never heard a single girl from our class brag or boast about Laine until after our encounter.

"There's something I need to ask you."

"Anything."

"Was I your first?"

His cheeks give him away. "Yeah, but you weren't the last girl I've been with if that makes you feel any better."

"Why would that make me feel better?"

"Cause, you know, I've improved since then." He blushes.

"I didn't ask because I thought you sucked in bed."

"Then how did you know?"

"You'd go mute when the guys started talking about who they were banging."

"Maybe I'm just a gentleman."

"It wasn't just you. None of the girls at school ever talked about sleeping with you." I move into his personal space. I want to be in his space, I want him in mine. "You are definitely worth bragging about." I back him up until he's sitting on the bed.

"It wasn't like I didn't have a chance before you. I don't know. I wanted it to be special, to mean something." He has no clue how special he is and how honored I am to have been his first. What we shared had nothing to do with Benny. Everything that happens from this moment forward is about us.

Laine's hand slowly creeps up the back of my thigh. I fall onto him and he flips me to my back. His stubble tickles my chin as his lips move down my neck. He slowly works his way to my collarbone and back.

Maybe Benny was the catalyst who brought us together. Maybe it was Bryn. Everything about Laine—his eyes, his lips, his room—it feels like I belong here. I want to belong here. I want to belong to Laine.

He finishes undressing me, and I lay beneath him waiting to feel his warmth against my body. This isn't about revenge or hurting Benny. We're just two people who want each other.

He pulls his boxers off, and I lean forward unwilling to allow any space between us. I hook my arms under his and pull him back down to me. My mouth meets the hollow space at the base of his neck.

"Wait." He reaches across the bed to his nightstand. He slides open a drawer and pulls out a silver square. He rips it open and slips the condom on. I wait for him to make the next move but he remains still.

Are you...ready?" I feel like an idiot as soon as the words leave my mouth.

"I just want to savor every second of this."

"You make me sound like a piece of cake."

"That's exactly what you are." He kisses my neck. "Sweet." He runs his tongue from my shoulder to my ear lobe. He takes it into his mouth, and I moan. "Decadent," he whispers as his hand runs over my breasts. He rubs it gently, then moves lower. When his fingertip dips between my legs, I grab his bicep and close my eyes. "And creamy."

"Do you always play with your food?"

He slides his hand from between my legs and lowers his body until he's resting against me. "Only the things I rarely get to enjoy."

"And how often do you enjoy cake?" I narrow my eyes as if I'm jealous and suddenly it feels real. Laine smiles at the heat rising in my face. He can read the tension in my eyes. I love it. I love every second of being with him. He gets me.

"I don't have cake very often. In fact, it's been months."

"Well, I hope you enjoy this cake because it's the only cake you're going to eat for a while."

HEY, BABE
Chapter Seven

Laine likes to kiss in inconvenient places. One step above me on an escalator, in a revolving door. Kissing him is never boring. We have become that disgustingly happy couple who sits on the same side of the table at restaurants. We hold hands and share our food. I've become everything I thought I hated. Matching shirts, finishing each other's sentences. Calling each other *babe*. He's strong in a way I can never be. He keeps the darkness at bay. With him by my side, I can get through anything.

We arrive at Yerba Buena Gardens for the free concert series and spread out a blanket near the stage. Laine is lying on his back; my head is resting on his stomach, our bodies forming a T. I sip on a venti iced coffee as we listen to a twelve-year-old girl play 1990s rock on her violin. Just as the first chords of Radiohead's "Creep" fill the air, Misty sits down beside us.

"Hey, Laine," she says. "What's going on?"

"S'up, Misty." He tilts his head back and smirks. "There's a concert going on." He tangles his fingers with mine as if to show Misty he isn't alone.

Misty pulls out her phone.

I sit up. "Is there something you want to ask before you go all paparazzi on us?" I contemplate how quickly I could snatch the phone from her hand and chuck it into the Martin Luther King memorial fountain.

"I'm not going to take your picture," Misty snaps. "I don't give a shit who you fuck, but Laine you really should know better."

"Whoa." Laine sits up.

"I'm just saying, rolling with your best friend's leftovers." Misty starts typing a text. "You're so much better than…that." She twirls her pointy finger in my direction.

"You can't sit here and insult my girlfriend," Laine stands.

"Girlfriend?" I repeat. We've been dating close to three months, but we haven't slapped a label on it.

"I don't know, yeah. I guess. Don't you think?" He smiles with his whole face.

"I mean, yeah." I squeal because I can't hold in my emotions a second longer. I bounce into his arms, and he swings me around while the violin wails.

"Does Benny know?" Misty just *has* to ruin the moment.

"Benny lives on the other side of the country." Misty knows he's going to school in New York, she's an Instagram stalker.

"And even if he were here, he wouldn't care." Laine looks at me and smiles. "He knows about us."

"I thought I was just a dirty little secret."

"He's my best friend," Laine says sarcastically. "I tell him everything." He leans down and kisses me in front of Misty, in front of everyone.

"You guys are perfect for each other." Misty stands and stomps away.

"Yeah, we know," Laine yells at her back. "She's also the first girl I had sex with!" Everyone within hearing distance looks our way, except Misty. "Ladies and gentlemen, the girl who won my virginity." Laine presents me to the crowd and I curtsy. A few people clap while others turn back to the stage.

"You are nuts," I tell Laine as we sit down.

"We're nuts," he corrects.

I know, and it's fucking beautiful.

When the concert is over, we go back to my house. I'm still on a high as I walk through the door, but it diminishes the moment I see her. Laine pushes past me and runs to the spot where my mother is passed out on the floor.

"She's drunk," I tell him.

"Should I help her?" He waits for my instructions.

I run to my room.

Laine comes in a few minutes later. "I put her in bed."

"She gets stressed about work and stuff...she isn't always like this."

"You don't have to explain, baby." He takes off his shoes and lays beside me so we're face to face. Laine wipes runover tears from my nose with his sleeve. "I think I'm in love with you."

"Well, I know I'm in love with you."

He breaks into a grin then leans forward to kiss me. My lips part and I taste remnants of the chocolate ice cream we ate on the way home.

"I'm gonna get you out of here." Even Laine feels the hopelessness of this place. "I'm just waiting for my job with the city to come through. It's a union job with good pay and benefits. I'll make enough so we can afford an apartment." Laine sits up with an enthusiastic burst of energy. "I know we're young, but I also know this is real." He cups my face. "I plan to take care of you for the rest of my life." He slides off the side of my bed onto his knees. "Will you marry me?"

I choke, literally, and run to the bathroom. I don't puke. I don't cry, but I'm scared. I want this to be real. I want Laine to say things that are real. Marrying me is a fairytale—and not the good kind. It's lofty and childish to believe we're ready for that kind of commitment. Kissing in the park and sharing ice cream cones is good enough for me. That's the kind of love I want with Laine. Not marriage and rent.

When I return, Laine is sitting with his head in his hands. "I'm sorry," he says. "I thought...."

I drop to my knees in front of him. "I love you, Laine. And I will spend the rest of my life loving you. I just don't think I'd make a very good wife."

"I don't want a good wife." He kisses my forehead. "I want you." He cradles me in his arms. "I want you, forever."

It is at this moment, sitting on the unvacuumed floor in my room, that I stop holding on to the pain. I let it go and give myself completely to Laine. "You're going to be the love of my life, aren't you?"

"Goddamn right, I am."

"Then I guess I have to marry you."

YOUNG, DUMB AND BROKE

Chapter Eight

TWO YEARS LATER

Somewhere between the ages of eighteen and twenty, your life begins. Whether you're away at college or bumming around your parents' house, you realize shit is getting real. Sleeping until noon makes you feel lazy. Not having enough money for a movie ticket and a bag of popcorn sucks. Knowing you are solely responsible for someone else's happiness keeps you up at night.

Laine is always worried. He eats more, runs more, we have sex less. Money is the main topic of all our conversations. When I suggest we get a cone at Mitchell's, he tells me there is ice cream in the freezer. When I'm craving tomato soup in a bread bowl from Boudin, he hands me a can of Campbell's and a bag of white bread. When we're about to have sex and Laine reaches into the drawer and finds his box of condoms is empty, he tosses me my clothes.

"What's going on with you?" I ask as I angry dress. "It's not a big deal."

"Getting pregnant isn't a big deal?"

It freaks me out when he says the p-word—even *thinking* it is bad luck. We had one close call a year ago; it was the most stressful week of our lives. We can barely support ourselves. Who am I kidding, we don't support ourselves. Laine is still on the list for the city job. His father is certain his name will be pulled soon. Soon isn't a guarantee, it isn't a certainty. Soon is bullshit.

Laine's parents don't like me. Benny's mother was gracious enough to inform Laine's mom of my history with her son. As if a high-school romance matters in the grand scheme of things. If we were judged by the people we dated, or the people we were in high school, the world would be a seriously fucked up place.

The DiCaro's tolerate me because Laine loves me. They trust his judgment and assume I'm a somewhat acceptable companion for their son. If they knew about my mother's drinking, they'd probably ban me from the house.

I take my time with each shoe, retying the laces so they are just right, hoping Laine will stop me. I don't want to leave. I never want to leave him but I won't stay unless he asks, nicely. My plan is backfiring because I'm fully dressed in perfectly tied shoes and Laine is still staring at the ceiling.

"I'm going home."

"Wait."

Phew!

I pause with my hand on the door and turn around with a scowl on my face. It'll fade as soon as he apologizes. I can never stay mad at him for long.

"Your keys." He points to my house keys on the desk.

I snatch them and walk out, leaving his bedroom door open. Nobody is home. We only have sex when nobody is home because that is our life. I walk down the hall and out the door, letting it slam behind me. Something has been bothering Laine for weeks. I thought maybe he was seeing someone else, but I've been monitoring his social media. I even check his phone when he's in the bathroom. I haven't found any evidence he's cheating, which makes me feel even shittier for snooping.

I get home and find my mom painting the dining room tea green. She claims it's calming. *Whatever.*

"I picked up ravioli from Lucca's. It's in the fridge if you're hungry."

"I'm not hungry." Unlike Laine, food doesn't comfort me. I shut my bedroom door and kick off my shoes. I fall face-first into my faded gray comforter wishing I hadn't left Laine. Running home isn't how adults deal with life. One day, we'll have our own place. Our own condoms. Once the city job comes through. It pays well, which is why it's so hard to get in. The only time a position opens is when someone leaves or gets fired. Last month one of the low-level guys was caught drinking a beer in a work truck. There were fifty-two people in line for his job. Even with Laine's father on the inside, he only moved up to number eighteen.

Laine gave up going to college because his father convinced him he could get a job with the city. He said accruing one hundred thousand dollars in student loans wouldn't help him in this economy. If he actually came through with the job, his father would be right. Until that day comes, Laine is stuck working shit jobs for shit pay. He doesn't want to push a broom or bag groceries. Laine wants to make a difference. San Francisco Municipal Works is part of the city's first responders. In the event of an earthquake or terrorist attack, Laine would be dispatched to check water mains and gas lines. He likes that aspect of the job. It's the only thing he likes and the sole reason he's still waiting.

A year ago, when Laine thought he was six months from the city job, we started looking for apartments. He even borrowed his mother's car and we drove out to IKEA. We spent five hours playing house. I made a list of all the things we envisioned having in our home. A funky red sofa and a shaggy green rug. I look at the list taped to my wall, just above the list I made with Bryn. They're both bucket lists when I think about it. Both made with people I love.

"Alee." Mom knocks once then opens my door. "Laine is on the phone." Mom has been sober for eleven weeks. She's going to slip soon. Painting is the first sign.

"Why is he calling the house phone?"

"I don't know." She shrugs and walks away, leaving my bedroom door open.

Mom replaced the cordless kitchen phone with an old-school model with a twisty cord that hangs on the wall. She thinks it's retro. It's really just cheap as fuck.

"Hello," I sigh.

"Hey, babe," he says in a voice that makes me want to scream.

"What?"

"You left your phone here." His tone is soft, loving. I want him to be a prick so I can stay mad.

"So."

"I just wanted you to know before you tore up your room looking for it."

"Okay."

Silence.

"Do you want me to bring it over?" Which translates to I'm ready to apologize for being a prick.

"Don't do me any favors."

"Come on, Alee."

"What?"

"I'm sorry. I was just frustrated."

"About what?"

"About not being able to afford a box of condoms," he snaps. "I just want to get to the next part of our lives. I want to hit that next level."

"Yeah, me too." I don't mean it. Seventy-five percent of the things I say are lies. The next level doesn't exist. We are where we are. There is no invisible ladder, no elevator to the top. It's just him and me. Existing.

"I'd like to come over, Alee."

I don't want to see him right now. I want to lie in my room and stare at the ceiling. This is my safe place. I know every inch of the room by heart. The water stain in the corner shaped like the letter P. The guts of a spider I smashed on the door two—no, three years ago. The weathered poster my mother hung above my bed to help me sleep when I was seven. Like most of my mom's ideas, it was bad. I blamed my insomnia on those creepy numbered sheep. I've lived my entire life within these four walls. I don't want to die here. My only hope for escaping this place is Laine. We're a team no matter what.

"Okay," I say because I have to. Telling Laine not to come over means more than I'm tired or still angry. Telling him to stay away means I have issues with him, our relationship, the world. He's the last person I want to push away. He is my world.

BLACK EYES ARE SEXY

Chapter Nine

Laine applies for seven jobs and gets no call-backs. His dad is constantly in his ear telling him the city job will open up soon. Nobody believes it anymore. I have a part-time job at a bakery on Valencia Street where I sell baked goods and pour coffee. Mostly, I bus tables. Aside from the nine dollars an hour, I also get free bread. Laine loves the ciabatta. He says I'm making him fat, but I don't care. I like seeing him happy. Bread makes him happy.

My phone buzzes just as my shift ends. It's Laine; he's waiting for me at Dog Eared Books down the street. I clock out, grab a loaf of ciabatta, then head to find my love. I see him when I'm half a block away. He's looking into the window of the bookstore and doesn't acknowledge the two giggling girls staring at him.. I feel like letting the little sluts know he's mine, but I don't. I just smile, knowing I'm the one who gets to kiss him whenever I want.

"Hey, sexy." I push up onto my tiptoes to kiss the back of his neck. He turns around, holding his eye. His shirt is torn and splattered with blood. "What happened?" I scan the block to see if anyone is lying unconscious nearby.

"Just some asshole," he says. "I didn't want to show up to your work looking like this."

"Do we need to get out of here?" I look around for cops.

"No, it happened an hour ago."

"Jesus Christ, Laine! You should've gone home." I take his elbow and start towards the bus stop.

"I don't want my mom to see me like this."

"Should we stop by Saint Luke's?"

"Nah, I'm good. I just need to get cleaned up."

We go to my house since Mom is at work. Not that my mom would care. She isn't the nurturing, hovering type. I convinced myself it was a good thing because I had freedom. Nobody breathing down my neck if I forgot to do my homework or got detention. Nobody waiting up for me at night. Nobody who cared. Being around Laine's family sort of changed my perspective. It's nice to know somebody in the world gives a shit if you make it home alive. At least I have Laine now. He's my somebody.

"There's an ice pack in the freezer," I tell him as I go to the bathroom for the first aid kit and a washcloth. We meet on the living room sofa.

Laine pulls his shirt off. I pour a little hydrogen peroxide on the cloth to clean the blood around his nose. He winces, and I notice his top lip is busted. He brings the ice pack to his eye, and I see the blood splatter on his forearms.

"What does the other guy look like?"

"Bloody." His voice is nasally as he tells me what happened. "I got off the 24-line, and this asshole was riding by on one of those motorized scooter things. He almost hit a pregnant lady stepping out the back door. I yelled for him to slow down. Actually, I called him an asshole and told him to slow down."

I smile and rub my hand on his bare chest. He's such a hero.

"Anyway, the dickhead comes back around and gets in my face. So I head-butted him. That's how this happened." He points to his nose and his bruised eye. "I was off a little."

"And this." I point to the blood on his arms.

"I punched his face a few times before a couple of guys pulled me off. That's how my t-shirt ripped."

I love that he stood up for that pregnant woman. If he's willing to protect a random stranger on the street, imagine what he would do to protect the people he loves.

77

"Anyone would've done the same."

"No, they wouldn't" I set the cloth on the coffee table and straddle his lap. "The black eye is turning me on." I kiss his swollen lip. He winces at first, then flips me onto my back.

"We've never had sex on this couch." Laine has one knee on the sofa, between my legs; his other knee is on the floor. He unsnaps the top of his jeans and smiles. His teeth are blood-stained and his eye is almost swollen shut. He's a mess. But he's my mess. I taste blood when we kiss, his blood. "I love you so much."

He kisses my neck, then pulls my t-shirt off. He starts to tug on my jeans when he remembers. "I don't have any condoms."

I fall onto the sofa and look at the ceiling in exasperation. "I should just go on the pill."

"No." He sits up. "It makes you sick."

"I can try another brand."

"You've tried four already. It isn't worth it."

Nausea and vomiting would start about thirty minutes after I take it and lasted up to six hours kind of like food poisoning. My doctor says it happens with some women. I tried the patch, too. When that didn't work, Laine said he had no problem using condoms. The only problem: we run out often.

I trace the outline of Laine's chest muscles. I'm not giving up that easily. I climb back onto his lap. He unhooks my bra and tosses it on the floor, then pulls me against his shirtless body. I rest my head on his chest to absorb his heat.

"I want to marry you, Alee. I want to start a family. I want to grow the fuck up already."

We're not ready to be married. Emotionally, yes. To my utter dismay, love isn't all you need. There is a lot more to being married than a wedding. Laine's vision of our wedding day does not match mine. He wants to celebrate our union with the world. I'm the opposite. This is between him and me. I'm afraid to let the universe know how happy I am. Life has a way of balancing itself out. When you start showing off, life bites back.

"Let's go to City Hall and do it right now."

I kiss his neck and imagine the amazing honeymoon sex we will have.

"I have some money saved. We can get a hotel downtown and be as loud as we want." Laine pulls me close. It feels good. We never get to share moments like this. Even our sex is rushed or hushed, depending on the time of day or who is home.

"If we go to City Hall and get married today"—I smile at the idea—"where would we live? Married people generally share the same address." Even though we're always together, we don't officially live together. "It makes the most sense to live here." I answer my own question just for the sake of conversation. Playing the what-if game is one of our favorite pastimes. "There are fewer people."

"And what happens when your mom slips again?"

"I'll deal with it, same as always." Suddenly my mother on a binge seems less stressful than living under the scrutiny of Laine's parents. The idea of being in the same space as my mother twenty-four/seven isn't ideal but living with his parents would kill me.

"My house is bigger, and we wouldn't have to share a bathroom."

"I can't breathe at your house." I give the look. The one I use every time his father makes a snide remark about my employment, or my hair, or my lack of motivation.

"They don't hate you, they just want…more from me."

"Better for you."

"You make me a better man. I wouldn't be holding out for this job if it weren't' for you. The city job means stability and good money. We're going to have an amazing life, Alee. I don't want to wait another day."

Laine and I have lots of plans. Plans I feel will never come to fruition. We're always waiting. Waiting for someone else to come through so our lives can begin. At what point do we start forging our own path, creating our own fate? Maybe that starts with a wedding. My fingers graze his chest. I look at him in awe. I get to touch that chest. Rub those abs. Kiss that neck. Laine is mine. All mine. Forever. His gentle touch and his sweet voice are all that matters. Where we live is irrelevant as long as we're together.

"Okay," I concede.

"Okay, what?"

"Okay, we can live at your house."

The elation on Laine's face can carry me through the next few months of torture I will suffer under his parents' roof. It's worth it. *He is worth it.*

Laine makes love to me on my mother's sofa. We don't think of the consequences, just each other.

LAUNDRY DAY
Chapter Ten

I happen upon Hawk as he is dragging a black trash bag into the laundry mat on Valencia. I offer to buy him breakfast, but he opts for a coffee and bagel from the corner store instead. Hawk seems distant lately, like meeting me is an inconvenience. He's the one who bailed on his family, the least he can do is pretend I matter, that I'm more important than laundry day.

"Do you always wash your clothes on Monday?"

"I wash when washing is necessary."

There are so many responses to that statement. Like could've fooled me or if that were true you wouldn't smell like the dumpster behind the taqueria.

"I have a pair of jeans that I've never washed. I just Febreze them every now and then." Sometimes I say things to find commonality with Hawk. I usually just come off sounding like an idiot.

Hawk nods like he uses Febreze all the time. For him to buy a bottle of air freshener is a frivolous splurge, sort of like how I feel about meth.

Hawk washes his clothes in hot water, rinses in cold, and adds fabric softener to the rinse cycle. Homeless people use fabric softener—who knew? I say little the entire time his clothes are laundering. We've been meeting long enough for me to know when Hawk doesn't feel like making small talk.

After the laundromat, we walk down Valencia towards the freeway. The stench of the place hits me before I see it. The homeless encampment is huge and sits under the freeway on Division Street. It's only a matter of time before the cops make a sweep. Hawk says it can happen day or night. When they come, he only has a few minutes to get his things and run. He considers himself lucky. He has only lost everything he's ever owned twice—the day he left his family and the day he left Portland. He equates losing a shopping cart in a police raid to abandoning his family. It's nice to know I mean as much to him as a piss and shit-stained sleeping bag.

"Why do you want to live like this?" We walk past rows of dirty tents and carts stacked with cardboard and cans. I'm met with cautious glares, while my father is greeted with love and respect. The world is upside down in this place. My

Old Navy coat is too new, my hands and nails too clean. In this camp, people are judged by their scars. Just because I don't cloak mine in dirt or flaunt them with booze and drugs doesn't mean they don't exist.

My father has a small gray and blue dome-shaped tent, the kind seen on the cover of an outdoor magazine. He unzips it, then reaches in and pulls out a bag.

"Nobody bothers me here."

I cringe feeling like that was directed at me.

He starts repacking his duffel, the same duffel he left with when I was four. "People have unrealistic expectations of each other. Especially when it comes to people we love." He zips the clothes he just washed at the laundromat into the bag and slings it over his shoulder. The bag says PROPERTY OF SAN FRANCISCO GENERAL HOSPITAL on the side.

I think about Benny. He always talked about working at SF General. He said they'd name a wing after him someday. I wonder where Hawk's bag came from. Did he work at the hospital? Was he a patient?

"At some point, Alee, you have to start living for you."

"That's why you gave up on us?" I didn't mean to say us, as in Mom and me. It just slips out, and I can see it affects him. The more time I spend with my father, the softer I feel. Like all the parts of me that were angry about not having him in my life no longer exist. I know now that I didn't need this man around. I may even be glad that he wasn't in my life. An addict isn't a father, but I still find myself wishing he would get his life together so I could have one. "You didn't want to be around me anymore?" I shouldn't push too far. The last time our conversation turned heavy I didn't see him for a month. I'm crumbling his wall too. "You didn't want to be a father or a husband. You chose this over your family."

"I understand why you see it that way. I didn't give up on you or her. I gave up on me. I gave up being the person who let you guys down."

I inherited so much more than his eyes and smile. He hides from life in a homeless camp and I hide in my mother's house.

"I wanted you, Alee, and I wanted your mom. But what I want and what I could offer were two very different things. Once I realized I could never be the man your mother needed, the kind of father you deserved, well the choice was simple. Some people are good at math; some can hot-wire a car. One person isn't better than the other because one lives a straight, clean life. Maybe this is what I'm meant to do. I mean, shit, I've lasted this long." He looks around the camp as if he's soaking it all in. He's in his element. "We're strong people, me and you. When our haters go to their graves, they'll wish they lived life like us."

If I'm like him, does that mean what I have with Laine won't last? Will I abandon him with a kid? Do I even want kids? I second guess the life I see with Laine. I second guess life in general.

"I gotta go, Alee." Hawk cups the side of my face. "You take care." His eyes gloss over as he backs away and disappears into the crowd.

I go home and check the mirror; my father's dirty fingerprint sits on my left cheek. I leave it there for two days.

I'M THE BUM

Chapter Eleven

We go to Laine's house for Sunday dinner. Without warning me, he tells his parents we have big news. The relief on his mother's face when Laine jokingly says, "Don't worry, we're not pregnant," makes me cringe. I realize at this moment just how much they hate me.

"We're getting married." Laine puts his arm around my chair and kisses my head. The sweet gesture causes him to miss the vein that pops out on his father's right temple. I will never understand how this man ended up with such a kind-hearted son.

Tears fall when Janey learns we plan to marry at City Hall. "Laine, please," she says. "Think of your future."

"What future?" he snaps, then recoils quickly. He never raises his voice to his mother. "I love Alee. I'm going to marry her with or without your blessing."

"Where will you live?" His father, James, looks at me with so much hate in his eyes, it feels like his hand is squeezing my heart.

"If we can't live here, then we'll live at Alee's house." Laine grips my sweaty hand in that I-got-you way.

"You think getting married will make you a man?" James snaps. "You're still living off other people." He walks across the room and opens the window. It's suddenly very hot in their dining room. He turns around, and his eyes fall to me. "What about you?" he says. "Are you looking for a real job, a career? What do you bring to the table?"

I'm afraid to speak. If I do, horrible things will fly from my lips. Words that can't be taken back or forgiven.

"Don't speak to her in that tone," Laine warns his father. "At least she has a job. What do I have, Dad? I'm a bum. She shouldn't want me."

I run my hand down his arm. We both know that isn't true. He does side work with his cousin's construction company, and he volunteers at the Boys & Girls Club. He's an assistant basketball coach and helps run the after-school program.

"She waits tables." James looks at me. "Is that your plan? Are you going to pour coffee for the rest of your life?"

I open my mouth but just air comes out.

"She'll be the mother of my children," Laine announces. His mother sobs even louder, and his father walks out of the room. Laine follows, then Janey. They congregate in his parent's bedroom, right next to the dining room. Even with the door closed, I make out bits and pieces of their conversation.

She's trash.

Her mother is a drunk.

You're too good for her.

The door flies open and hits the wall. Drawers bang, another door slams closed. I can't tell who is slamming and banging, the only discernable sound is crying.

Laine reappears with a carry-on bag on his shoulder.

"Let's go to your place."

I enter the hall feeling James and Janey watching us. Laine doesn't pause, we walk out with no intention of going back

***

Within the first two weeks of living at my house, Laine fixes the leaky kitchen sink, replaces the burnt out light bulbs in the dining room chandelier, paints the trim around the living room windows, and hangs the spice rack Mom bought three years ago. I never asked if Laine could move in. I didn't think I needed to. Plus, he's like a live-in handyman. And he cooks. My mother stays hidden in her room. She's not quite sober, not binging. Laine is very polite; I think it freaks her out. Our home is the only place neither of us has to pretend. We can be shitty and fucked up—you know, our real selves. With Laine here, she isn't sure it's safe.

We decide to get married on Laine's twenty-first birthday. It's six weeks away, and we're hoping he lands a job by then. Laine says he won't tell his parents or any of his cousins. It's our secret. Our day. There isn't anyone we can invite who would make the day any more special.

On Friday night, Laine gets a call from his father. He asks him to come over for dinner, alone. Laine protests at first, but I convince him it's better this way. It will give them time to hash out their family issues. He leaves at six o'clock and ends up staying the night. I don't realize it until my alarm goes off a four-thirty in the morning. I call him on my way to work and it goes to voicemail.

Now I'm worried.

What could his parents have said or done to turn Laine against me? He wouldn't leave me. He promised. I'm frantic by the time my first break comes. When I see a text from Laine, I'm almost too scared to check it. I call him instead.

He doesn't say hello when he answers. I hear him moving, then a door closes. "Sorry, I didn't call."

"Laine, are you okay?"

"My mom has ovarian cancer. She's having surgery in two days. She needs me." He asks me not to come over, or go to the hospital. He says she just wants family around.

I tell him I understand. "Are you staying there?"

It sounds so lame, so selfish to even ask.

"Yes, she needs me. She's my mother."

"Of course. Well, call me when you can."

"Okay. Bye."

He didn't say he loved me.

By the third day, I miss him so much I can barely get up in the morning. I keep telling myself this wouldn't be happening if we had a place. If we lived on our own, he would come home. He'd come back to me. We're waiting for Laine's big career break, but what about me? James is right, I bring nothing to the table.

I apply for three jobs and land an interview. I don't tell Laine in case nothing comes of it. He doesn't need any added disappointment in his life.

Laine calls the day after his mother returns home. They're confident she'll be okay. He talks about working with his father again. We don't talk about getting married at all.

"I miss you," he finally says. "Can I come over tonight?"

"Yes, hurry." I hang up and do a quick sweep of my room. Tossing clothes into the basket and ice cream cartons in the trash. I shower and shave the important areas.

Laine arrives forty-five minutes later with a pizza from Haystacks and an extra-large box of condoms. If that isn't love, I don't know what love is.

HE'S THE BAD GUY
Chapter Twelve

Hawk doesn't show for our Thursday meeting.

I didn't expect him to be here, not after our last encounter. I decide to hang out at the spot and wait anyway. This is my place now. Regulars say what's up when they see me on the wall like I belong here. Even the birds recognize me.

I open the bag of Doritos I brought to share with my dad and feed them to the birds, my friends.

Laine still doesn't know about Hawk. I haven't told anyone because they wouldn't understand. Hawk is right, people have expectations. Laine will ask questions, he'll worry. Hawk doesn't just look like a street thug, he is one.

My father is the man who robs you in a dark alley, breaks into your car, beats you for a cell phone. He's a bad guy. At least he owns it. Unlike my mom who pretends to be more than a drunk. If I needed Hawk, like really needed him, he would have my back. That's what guys like him are good for. He'd kill for me.

CHANGE OF PLANS
Chapter Thirteen

It's Laine's birthday. We're celebrating at a bar called Greenberg's. I made a Facebook event and invited everyone on his friend's list. Even Benny. Thankfully, he's still in New York. He told Laine they'll celebrate next week at his welcome-home party. Only Benny would make Laine's birthday about him.

Benny turned twenty-one a month ago. His Instagram and Facebook posts hijacked my newsfeed for two days. He offered to fly Laine to New York for the weekend, but Laine declined. There was no point; Laine wasn't old enough to get into the bars and clubs Benny was name-dropping. I think the real reason he didn't go was me. I love him for that.

I walk out of my room in a pair of black jeans with tiny slits on the thighs, a blue tank top with a faded picture of Bob Marley, and a pair of knee-high boots. I used a wand on my hair to give it a little more wave and had my makeup done at the MAC store downtown. My outfit and makeup were paid for with my first paycheck. As of two weeks ago, I am an employee of the State of California. I'm the not-so-friendly face who collects your six dollars to cross the Bay Bridge into San Francisco. I'm the motherfucking gatekeeper.

Laine was happy for me, *is* happy for me. But my employment makes his part-time job at the sandwich shop on Church Street even more inadequate—his words, not mine. The guy who owns the deli is a friend of his father's, so Laine considers it charity. It's just something to hold him over until his city job comes through, which Laine's father claims is only months away.

His parents set up a household fund for Laine so he can buy groceries and take care of minor expenses that come up while his mother is recovering. It's also a way for them to give Laine money. He hates using the household fund for anything personal. It bothers me, too. Just knowing our condoms were paid for by his parents kills the mood.

That won't be an issue anymore. Now that I'm gainfully employed, I can afford condoms, clothes, and soon, our own place. I'm making decent money for someone with no real skills or a college degree. Laine respects the hell out of me, but he's also a guy, the kind who believes a man should support his woman. Once we're on our own, the pressure from his family will be off his shoulders. When his city job does come through, we'll get married, and finally make it to that next step Laine has been longing for.

Laine didn't actually want a party, but I insisted. We haven't gone out since I started my job. I work full-time, with another hour and a half commute. Laine only works four hours a day, then he spends the rest of his time working out. He started to train for one of those obstacle races right after his mother's surgery. I figured it was just a way for him to blow off steam. He runs up to ten miles a day and spends another two hours on weights. By the time I get home, he's beat; we both are. Tonight's party is a chance for us to have some fun. I have a huge surprise set up for later. After the party, Laine and I will head to the Hyatt downtown for a night of loud, uninterrupted sex.

Laine whistles when I walk past the kitchen. "I'm the luckiest bastard in the world."

"You bet your ass you are."

I let him take me by the waist and press me against the wall. He cups my butt cheeks with both hands. "This ass is mine later."

"Whatever you say, birthday boy." His kiss smudges my lipstick and I don't care. "People are waiting for us."

He grumbles. "I just want to spend the night with you."

"You will, as soon as we hang out with twenty or thirty of your closest friends."

We get to Greenberg's around nine. I recognize a couple of guys from high school, his new gym friends, and some of his cousins. As soon as we sit down, a round of shots arrive at our table. Laine and I have been hanging out here for two years, and I've never been carded. Greenberg's is a neighborhood bar, if you have someone to vouch for you, it's all good. The bartenders won't let a little thing like the law get in the way of making money. I reach for a glass and the bartender, Steve, asks for my ID. I smile like he's joking but he blocks my hand from the tray.

"Um, shit." I pretend to look for a purse with an ID that doesn't exist. "I think I left my wallet at home."

"Come on, Steve. We come in here all the time," Laine interjects.

"Yeah, and I thought your big ass was twenty-one. She's gotta be younger than you." Steve stands behind my chair like he's going to drag it out the front door. "Do you have ID or not, Alee?"

I look at Laine, then to Steve. "No."

Laine is about to stand up. I don't know if he plans to knock Steve out or walk me to the door.

"Ah, come on, Steve, let the little bird stay."

I cringe at the sound of his voice.

Laine looks past me towards the door then rushes to his best friend. "What the fuck are you doing here!"

They hug and the rest of the bar welcomes Benny home. Meanwhile, I think leaving isn't such a bad idea. I make my way to the door with Steve behind me.

"Hi, Ben," I say just to piss him off. He hates to be called Ben. It's either Benny or Benicio.

"Hey, little bird." He steps around Laine and gives me a kiss on the cheek. "You look beautiful."

It feels weird to hear Benny call me little bird. It's something he used to say when we were dating because "Three Little Birds" was my favorite Bob Marley song and my last name is Finch.

"Should we tell her?" Steve consults with Benny. "I'm starting to feel bad."

"The whole ID thing was your idea?"

"Yeah, just a little joke." Benny winks.

I want to slap the smug off his face, but it wouldn't matter. Smug is part of Benny's DNA.

We return to our table, and Steve brings a free round of shots. Then another. After the fifth, I start to get dizzy. I go to the bathroom to check my makeup. It's still flawless and totally worth seventy-five dollars. So far, everything has been perfect. Benny is sitting on the opposite side of the table and hasn't spoken to me all night. Laine is smiling a lot.

In an hour I'll order an Uber to take us to the hotel for some much needed sexy time.

"You okay?" Benny blocks me from exiting the bathroom.

"I'm fine," I slur and stumble around him.

He leads the way back to our table, pausing at the dartboard. "You want to play a round?" Benny taught me to play darts in his father's man cave. I was getting pretty good before we broke up.

"Sure." *One game won't hurt.*

We choose our darts and decide to play Around the Clock. We have to hit every number on the board in no particular order.

"So, how is New York?" I ask because small talk makes the fact that I'm playing darts with my ex a little less weird.

Benny throws his first dart and hits twenty. "The city is insane. There's always someplace to be. And the food is killer. You'd love it." He steps to the side so I can take my shot. My dart barely lands on the board.

"I'm a little rusty."

Benny smiles and tells me to take the next turn. "Laine told me about your job. Congratulations."

"Thanks." I throw my dart and hit nineteen.

Benny makes a face like he's impressed as I step aside.

"So, do you know what's going on with Laine?" He throws his dart, and it hits the side of the board. "Damn. Choked on that one."

I line up to take my next shot. "He's just tired of waiting for the city job. Same as always." My dart hits the seven.

"It's more than that," Benny disagrees. "He's hiding something. I can tell."

"You haven't seen him in months."

"Yeah, but we talk every day." Benny's dart hits the nine. "Something is off. It's like he wants to tell me, then holds back. And it isn't his mom; it's something else."

Benny is right, but I don't tell him so. I don't say anything as I throw my dart and hit two. I move to the side so Benny can go, and catch Laine watching us from across the bar. He isn't smiling.

Benny hits eleven then steps aside.

I feel Laine's eyes on me as I line my dart up and let it fly. It lands directly in the center of the board. Bullseye.

"Hell yeah!" Benny cheers. Before I know what's happening, he grabs me in a bear hug and spins me around. When we come full circle, I scan for Laine. He slams a shot then walks out of the bar with his workout buddy, Liam.

Benny sets me down and lifts my chin, forcing me to look at him. "You always amaze me, Alee." The moment feels way too intimate.

"What are you doing?" I step back, and his hand falls to his side. "Are you trying to make Laine jealous?"

"No, but I have every right. He did steal my girl."

"I wasn't *your* girl." I squeeze the darts in my hand.

"I'm joking, Alee." Benny moves to take his shot. "You did fuck him while we were together, though." He looks at me and tosses his dart at the board. When it hits the bullseye I don't cheer. I'll never cheer for him. I drop my darts in the bucket and walk back to the table. I pour myself a beer from one of the pitchers. Liam's girlfriend, Kelly, smiles at me. I clink my glass with hers and take a huge gulp.

"It sucks trying to pretend everything is good, huh?" She looks out the window where Laine and Liam are talking on the street with a couple of guys from the gym. Laine spends most of his free time with these people, and I don't even know their names.

"What do you mean?" I look back at Benny. He's texting someone or probably posting something on Facebook. He is a social media whore.

"It's hard to pretend you aren't scared, that you'll be okay when they leave," Kelly's eyes are glossy as she unzips her purse and pulls out a pack of cigarettes.

I feel like I'm missing a huge piece to her story. More like she is assuming I know what she's talking about. "Is Liam going somewhere?"

Kelly sips her beer and sort of chokes. "Um, I thought… Oh, God. I'm drunk. Don't listen to me." She shakes her head. "Um, I'm going to smoke."

I have no clue what she was trying to say or not trying to say. Benny walks back to the table and sits down. I start to get up, he pulls my hand, and I fall back into my chair.

"Alee, wait. I'm sorry. I guess I was just…I don't know, jealous or something. I see you and Laine together, and part of me thinks it could've been me."

My heart stops.

"Benny, please don't say any more." I scoot my chair away. "We were just kids. What I have with Laine is real."

"I know, Alee. I just wish I had what you have."

"Why are you doing this right now, tonight? Are you really that selfish?"

Benny reminds me he's been gone for the last two years. This is the first time I've seen him since high school. Laine and Benny usually make it a boys night when Benny is home from school. I always had the impression he didn't want to see me, that he hated me. The feeling was mutual.

"Wait, Alee. Please let me say this."

I begrudgingly sit and finish off my beer. This encounter is killing my buzz.

"When Laine told me what happened between you guys, I was pissed."

"He was the one who told you we slept together?"

Laine is honest to a fault.

"He made me promise I wouldn't tell you it was him. I wanted to kick his ass. He offered to let me but it wasn't worth it."

What Benny means is that I wasn't worth it. I wasn't worth losing his best friend over. I get it, Laine is special, I'd forgive him anything too.

"The entire time I was in New York, I couldn't imagine you with him. Until tonight. I see the way you look at each other." Benny stares at my hands in silent contemplation. I curl my fingers into a ball, hoping he doesn't reach for me.

Benny's pain is evident and valid. He was betrayed by two people he cared about.

"I won't do anything to come between you." He holds his hand out. "Friends?"

I know it will make Laine's life a lot easier if we're cordial so I shake Benny's hand. "Friends."

I have no delusions about what this means. We'll be polite. Make small talk, endure each other. I will never actually be friends with Benny. Having a relationship with my ex, even if it's condoned by Laine, doesn't feel right.

Laine returns to the table and sits across from Benny and me. "We need to talk."

Laine's expression is dark. I try to lighten the mood.

"We're friends now," I babble. "Should we make up a handshake?" Neither men laugh.

Laine looks from his best friend to me. I wonder if the tense look in his eyes is actually jealousy. I inch my chair away from Benny.

"Dude, what's going on with you?" Benny gets right to the point.

Laine looks out the window at his gym buddies. Liam gives him a thumbs-up with his arm draped around Kelly. She waves at me before they disappear.

"Who are those guys?" Benny gestures to the window.

"They work out together," I tell him.

"That's another thing. When did you turn into a gym rat?" Benny pours himself a beer. "You hate that shit."

"He's training for a mud run. What's it called?" I pour myself another beer and Laine picks it up. He drinks the entire thing, then slams the glass upside down on the table. "I think you're cut off." I slide the pitcher away.

"I'm not really training for a Spartan Race," Laine finally says. "I lied and I'm sorry."

The words don't make sense, not coming from Laine. Even Benny seems perplexed. Laine doesn't lie or keep secrets from the people he loves, even when the truth hurts.

"Talk to me, man. I want to help you."

"There's nothing you can do." Laine leans back in his chair. Whatever he's been holding back is seeping through the cracks. I'm not ready for his honesty.

"Is it your job or…" Benny looks at me like I'm the only other problem in his life.

"Fuck my job. That shit is embarrassing. I quit today."

It isn't like Laine to quit anything. His father must be pissed. Maybe that's why Laine's acting so weird. His father's opinion means a lot to him.

"I can make some calls and get you a job in the mailroom at my father's firm," Benny offers. "I'll text him right now."

"No!" Laine yells. "I don't want a job in a mailroom. I sure as hell don't want to make sandwiches anymore." Laine takes a deep breath and says some words. Words that make no sense. Words that sound like he enlisted in the Marines. Laine's eyes never leave my face; he's waiting for me to react. I don't. I only want to hear real things. Truth. This can't be true.

"What the fuck, Laine!" Benny shouts, then calls him an idiot and asks him if he wants to die.

"I'll do four years. When I'm out, I can go into law enforcement. It's what I've always wanted to do anyway."

Laine and I have been dating for almost three years, and this is the first I've heard about him wanting to be a cop or a Marine.

"Let's talk about those four *short* years." Benny's cynicism won't deter Laine. His mind is made up. "Where will you spend that time? The Middle East? Africa? Syria? This country has a hard-on for war and you just became its first line of defense. I mean, fuck, you couldn't have joined the Navy?"

"You know me, Benny. I hate confined spaces. Remember that time you locked me in the trunk of your dad's car?" Laine tries to lighten the mood. It doesn't work.

"Don't go, man." Benny's head drops to the table like we're in grade school playing 7-up. He's waiting for Laine to tap his hand, to choose him. Laine has made a choice and it doesn't involve me or Benny.

Laine moves to the chair beside his best friend. "Dude, I'll get through it." He pats Benny on the shoulder and rubs the back of his head. "I bag 'em; you tag 'em."

Benny sits up and laughs. This must be some inside joke between them. He hugs Laine, and they exchange words I can't hear. When they break apart, Laine says, "I love you, bro."

They hug one more time, then Benny leaves. He doesn't say bye to me or anyone else in the bar; he just walks out the door.

I run to the bathroom and puke.

Laine and I walk around the city all night contemplating his new future. *Our new future.* We never make it to the hotel. At six in the morning, we jump in a cab and go to the beach. The sun rises behind us as we stare into the ocean. I haven't said much. I let Laine do all the talking. He feels the need to explain his choice. I haven't made dinner plans in the last two years without consulting Laine. He enlists in the fucking Marines without telling me. Without telling anyone.

The worst part: he leaves in a week.

One week.

I have seven days left with him. I don't want to spend that time fighting or crying. I don't want to think about what should've happened or what might happen. I just want to enjoy his smell, his touch, his kisses, before he's gone. I don't tell him about the hotel I wasted three hundred dollars on. I don't tell him I'm scared or mad, or disappointed. I smile and kiss his cheeks. I say everything will be okay and send Kelly a friend request on Facebook.

He wants me to keep working, save money, and when he's finished with basic training and infantry school, we'll decide where we're going to live. Of course, that all depends on where he is assigned. I don't understand the lingo, the acronyms, or the mindset that Laine has succumb to overnight. The one positive out of all of this is that Laine seems happier. The secrecy was killing him.

Until now, his only moral support has come from Liam. It turns out Liam and his gym buddies are actually fellow recruits. He enlisted right after his mother's surgery. He's been planning, training, all this time. He waited now to tell everyone because he knows we would've spent the last month trying to talk him out of it.

We take the N-train back to Castro Station and jump on the 24. I kiss him goodbye at the bus stop, then walk to my house. He's going to tell his parents. That is one conversation I'm happy to avoid. I go home and find my mom passed out on the couch. A bottle of bourbon sits on the table. She never fails to disappoint; it's the one constant in my life. I take a shower then head to bed. Before I close the blinds, I take the IKEA list off the wall and rip it up.

I SWEAR THESE DIRTY BIRDS RECOGNIZE ME

Chapter Fourteen

I sit on the concrete wall and crush a bag of chips. The sound is like a beacon. Birds swoop down from the tops of buildings and telephone poles, gathering around my feet in anxious anticipation. Some days I dump the entire bag and let them go at it. Today I scatter handfuls all around the station, so everyone gets a chance to eat. People sneer. A woman tells me the chips are bad for the birds. I don't care. The birds look happy.

The bag is empty, and two people have threatened to call the police on me for littering, so I decide to go. That's when I see my father's friend, Reginald. He's the quiet one and falls into the category of good people. When he stops to look through a discarded McDonalds bag, I ask him if he remembers me, and he mumbles yes.

I tell him it's been almost two months since I've seen Hawk. He says he's probably on a mission. That's what they call it when they binge. I ask Reginald to meet me next week, and he grumbles about not liking to be on a schedule. I promise him twenty dollars if he comes, and he agrees.

IT'S ALL OR NOTHING WITH ME

Chapter Fifteen

Everyone Laine has ever known calls, texts, or messages him on Facebook. They all want to say goodbye before he leaves. Laine refuses to make it a big deal. He tells them he wants to spend time with his family. They understand. Strangers are so fucking understanding.

Benny's parents insist on hosting a dinner for Laine. They invite his parents and a few of his cousins. When I walk into the Calderon's house, which has new hardwood floors and paint, Benny's mother, Beverly, forces a smile and kisses my cheeks like she's suddenly European. Benny's father shakes my hand. His name is Miguel, but he goes by Mike. That tells you a lot.

Miguel/Mike asks what I've been up to since I dumped his son. He doesn't actually say the last part, but his animosity is written all over his face. When I tell him about my job, he laughs. The motherfucker laughs. Then makes a remark about my job security since he read they're replacing the toll takers with machines. We're both surprised when Benny comes to my defense.

"Even if they put machines on the bridge, they'll still need someone to monitor them. What happens when an out-of-towner tries to drive through with no money? Someone will have to be there to let them through manually."

"That's true," Beverly agrees. "I always forget to carry change with me."

"You have FasTrak, Bev. Which proves my point." Miguel/Mike doesn't like to be challenged, especially by his wife. Beverly makes herself small again and sips her wine in silence.

A few minutes later, a server asks us to assemble in the dining room. A couple of bottles of wine are passed around the table as servers bring in platters of food. The Calderon's hired a chef to cater the meal. It's a bunch of fancy vegetables and sauces with names I can't pronounce. Most of it doesn't look edible. I'm not hungry anyway. I can't eat or sleep. I just lie awake and watch Laine. Sometimes his eyes pop open, and we stare at each other. In those moments I realize that he's going to miss me. He won't have me, the same way I won't have him. We lived for nearly eighteen years without each other. Now I can't bear to go eighteen hours without him.

After dinner we sit around the Calderon's living room, making small talk. Miguel/Mike has a friend who was in the Marines. Miguel/Mike has a friend who's done everything. He's that guy—the one-upper. He is telling Laine what to expect in basic training like he's been through it. I take a drink every time he says, "my friend." Within half an hour, I'm drunk. Benny must notice I'm a little crooked and suggests we get some air. It's raining outside, so we head downstairs to the man cave. A San Francisco Giants sign flashes in neon orange above the bar.

"That's awesome." I point to the sign.

"My dad has a friend…" He pauses. "Aren't you going to take a drink?"

"How did you know?"

"I've played that game many times." He turns on the speaker in the corner, then pulls his phone out to play music. "Remember, I know you, little bird."

"Don't call me that." I set my empty wine glass on the bar and pick up a set of darts.

"Sorry," Benny says without a trace of remorse as he opens the dartboard. "I can't be in this room without thinking of you, especially that couch."

I gave Benny my virginity on the black leather couch sitting smugly across the room. "Does it make you think of Bryn too?" I toss my first dart, and it hits just outside the bullseye.

Benny ignores my low-blow. "You always played better drunk." He sets a beer on the bar for me, knowing I won't drink it.

I toss another one; it hits off the board. "It's all or nothing with me."

"Yeah," Benny smirks. "I learned that the hard way."

I roll my eyes and walk to the board to retrieve my darts. Benny pulls another beer from the mini-fridge and opens it. He takes a pull and sits on a stool behind me. I toss two more darts and miss both times.

"I suck." I set the darts on the bar. "What did you learn the hard way?" I hate a small sip of the beer.

"If you don't love me, you hate me."

"I don't hate you."

"Does that mean you love me?"

I choke and spit the overpriced IPA all over Benny. He wipes his face and neck with one of the fancy cocktail napkins sitting in a neat pile on the bar.

This conversation is going down a dangerous path. I pick up the darts and turn back to the board. I toss one and miss.

"Do you at least like me?"

"What are you, twelve?" I miss another one. "Let's just say, I would cry if you died and leave it at that." I toss my last dart, it hits the side of the board and bounces back onto the bar.

"I can't take this." Benny moves behind me and aligns my body with the board. "Put your right foot forward." I move my foot. "Okay, now line it up." He holds my right hand with the dart in it. "You have to aim, Alee. You have to see where the dart is going."

"I never see where anything is going." I fling the dart; it goes high, hitting the twenty.

"I think you see things better than all of us." Benny moves back to the stool and picks up his beer. He considers what he's about to say. Then takes a drink. "You know I was in love with you." He points the beer bottle at me. "You broke my heart."

"I'm sorry," I murmur. "I'm sorry I hurt you."

"What you said that day, about me blocking the sun, I got it, Alee. And I'm working on it."

I need Benny to stop speaking. My heart is racing. How is Benny doing this to me? Or maybe I'm doing it to myself. What does my heart know, anyway? It knows this is wrong.

"Yo, Benny." Laine walks into the room, and his eyes fall to the darts in my hand. "What is it with you guys and darts?"

"It's our thing." Benny winks at me. I roll my eyes.

"It isn't like foreplay or something, is it?" Laine removes the darts from my hand. "Because I'm pretty sure I can take you, Calderon."

"No doubt, brother." Benny slaps Laine on the back. They break into matching smiles.

Laine and Benny play while I watch. They make small talk about boot camp and what Laine has planned for after.

"I'll do my infantry training at Camp Pendleton, then I get my orders." Laine tosses his last dart, then sits beside me on the leather couch. Visions of me and Benny dangle over his head and I internally slut-shame myself.

"What happens if you get sent to the Middle East?"

"Then I go to the Middle East." Laine kisses my head and pulls me close. "But I'll be back before then. I get leave after boot. I think ten days is more than enough time to get married." Laine's announcement causes Benny's dart to fly high and land in the wall. I feel dinner creep up my throat.

"Seriously?" I turn to face him.

"Yes, you're coming on this journey with me if that's what you still want. With your new job I understand if…"

"Fuck my job." I jump into his lap and kiss his face.

117

Benny clears his throat to get our attention. I don't give it to him. It isn't until I hear Laine's father in the hall that I break away.

"What are you boys doing down here?" He stops speaking when he sees me. It's like he forgot I was here. Even his sour face can't wipe away my smile.

"You're just in time for the good news," Benny smirks.

"What's that?" James leans against the bar.

Laine shoots a look at Benny then stands up. "I was just telling Benny my plans after boot." Laine moves to the bar and stands in front of his father. "During my ten-day leave, I'm going to marry Alee."

James looks at me with no contempt in his eyes. For once, I think he's happy Laine has me. "Congratulations, son."

"Thanks, Dad."

"Congratulations, Alee." He holds out his hand, and I stand up. He gives me a brief hug, then clears his throat. "Let's toast."

Benny pulls a bottle of tequila from the back of the bar and pours four shots. "To Laine and Alee."

We clink our glasses together, then toss back the warm alcohol. I make a sound of disgust, and Laine rubs my back.

"So, does this mean I get to throw a bachelor party?" Benny pours another shot for him and Laine.

I look at my fiancé and shake my head. "No."

Benny makes a disappointed face.

Laine shrugs. "She's the boss."

We leave Benny's and go back to my house. Mom is in her room. Laine heads to the bathroom while I go to the kitchen for water. I open the refrigerator, and the smell of hard-boiled eggs slaps me in the face. I can't stop the gag, and Laine is in the only bathroom, so I puke into the kitchen sink. As I dry-heave my dinner over a dirty cereal bowl, the light flickers on.

"Alee, are you okay?" My mother appears by my side, the smell of bourbon on her breath.

"Yes, I drank too much at dinner." I wave her away. The thought of wine and tequila makes me heave one more time.

She moves around the kitchen, then reappears with a bottle of water. I drink half of it, then vomit the water into the sink. I hear Laine's voice in the hall. They're whispering to each other. It pisses me off.

"Laine," I yell. "I'm fine. It was the tequila."

"Are you sure, Alee?" My mother hands me a can of Sprite. "You were sick last week."

I pop open the soda and take a small sip. The carbonation burns my throat. "That was bad Chinese food."

"When was the last time you had your period?"

The mention of my menstrual cycle freaks Laine out. "Are you saying she's pregnant?" He paces around the kitchen.

Mom looks at me with knowing eyes. My period is two weeks late, and I've been nauseated. I don't want to acknowledge the possibility. If the universe finds out I'm going to have Laine's child, it will somehow retaliate.

I'D DIE FOR
A CUPCAKE

Chapter Sixteen

Everyone in my life is gone.

It's just me and the birds, and Reginald.

The first few weeks, he's vague. I do most of the talking. I ramble about work and traffic. Reginald responds to everything I say with a slow nod or sometimes a smirk, good news or bad. He could care less about my pregnancy or upcoming nuptials. Reginald is just here for the money. During our fourth meeting, he asks if I want to know how he met Hawk.

"Sure."

"He beat my ass over a cupcake." He tries to laugh and chokes on his lunch. We're sitting on the wall eating burritos from the taqueria. Birds brawl at our feet for fallen rice and meat.

"A cupcake like with frosting?"

"Is there any other kind?"

"Must have been a pretty special cupcake."

"They give out freebies at that fancy pants bakery on Capp Street every night. You know, the ones they don't sell. If you think these birds are brutal, you should head down to the bakery around seven-thirty. That night, the night I met yo daddy, I waited two hours and scored the last one. I planned to eat it later, after dinner."

"Of course."

"I was headed to the park on Valencia when I ran into Hawk and his boys." Reginald looks up with an *oh fuck* look. "You don't want to run into that bunch day or night, not when you're carrying a fancy cupcake."

"What flavor?"

"What?"

"What flavor was the cupcake?"

"Chocolate."

"Why didn't you just give it to him?"

Reginald stands, burrito remnants scatter on the ground, the birds fly into a frenzy over fallen peas and rice. "It was my fucking cupcake!" He stomps towards his cart.

"Don't leave." I plead. "I was just trying to say a cupcake isn't worth a beating."

"Have you ever had a Capp Street Cupcake?"

"No."

He pushes his cart towards the park and grumbles something about me being a dumb bitch, and it was the principal of the matter, not the fucking cupcake.

"Same time next week?"

"Yeah, yeah."

"I'll bring cupcakes!"

Reginald is an addict too. According to him, that's all I need to know. It doesn't matter what walk of life you hail from when you're smoking crack, shooting heroin, or passing a bottle of cheap vodka, the playing field is leveled.

He won't let me call him Reggie. He also refuses to tell me his story. So I make shit up. With a name like *Reginald*, he probably had a lot to live up to, and that probably drove him to the streets. He's cleaner than my dad, which leads me to believe he hasn't been out here very long. His teeth tell another story. Several are broken or missing. When he chews, his lips curl inside his mouth. I buy him sandwiches from the deli so I don't have to sit across a table and watch him eat.

The following week I bring a dozen cupcakes. He eats two and saves the rest. He makes it clear that my grocery store bought confections aren't as good as the one he nearly lost an eye for.

"What's your last name, Reginald?" I ask knowing he won't tell me, but I have to try. I've considered trying to find his family. Anyone who could help him but I need his last name. "Did you grow up in the city?"

"Has anyone ever told you it's rude to ask a lot of questions?" Reginald is antsy today. "We got rules." He adjusts a plastic bag hanging on the side of his cart. A ratty sleeping bag drapes over the other side, covering his valuables: a pair of all-weather boots, the kind with fur around the ankle, and a down jacket. I've seen him in it a few times. A day pass for Heavenly Ski Resort hangs from the zipper. Everything Reginald owns was given to him by good Samaritans looking to fast track their way to heaven.

"I thought that was just in prison."

"You watch too much tv." He looks up into the trees that hover above 24th Street. "You're so keen on finding out how I got here but you never told me why you're doing this."

"Doing what?" I toss the remainder of my fries to the birds. I feed them twice a week now. The bird with one eye and half a leg will take a fry right out of my hand. Reginald thinks I'm going to catch some bird disease if it pecks me.

"Why are you here? It isn't my company. Don't you have a boyfriend?" This is the first personal thing he's ever asked me. Our conversations usually involve me trying to trip him up on information about my father.

"Are you offering," I tease.

"You don't know me. I could be a rapist." He grips the handles of his shopping cart and starts walking toward a garbage can.

"Are you?" I pause mid-step.

"No, but some of the people you talk to have done bad things." He stops and looks back at me. "I saw a guy dragging a woman into the park the other night. She was walking over there." He points to the park across the street then pushes his cart to the corner and looks through the trash can. He pulls out a plastic bag from a taqueria. He tucks it into his cart.

I pull my jacket tighter around my body. "Did you call the police?"

"Let me whip out my cell phone." He taps his pockets. "Plus, number one rule on the street, fuck that, in life, is you don't snitch." He points at me like I should write it down.

"Maybe the woman called for help...after."

"If you were raped by a homeless junkie, who would you call?" He picks up a Coke can and places it inside his cart.

My mother would never recover if something like that happened to me. "Nobody."

"I know."

"How do you know?" I challenge.

"If you had someone, you wouldn't be here with me."

Reginald grips the dirty handle on his shopping cart and starts down the street. I watch him hobble on his broken, duct-taped shoes and realize he is right.

.

UNEXPECTED PIZZA
Chapter Seventeen

Laine made me promise to document everything. My first doctor's appointment. My first craving. The first kick. His mother says I won't feel the baby move until my second trimester. Having my soon-to-be in-laws for moral support is great, but it isn't like having a friend. I have never missed Bryn as much as I do now. Laine's mom, Janey, is my go-to for baby questions. But when I'm missing Laine, there is only one person who understands what I'm going through

I pull out my phone and text Benny a series of sick emojis along with the middle finger. Benny writes back immediately with a sad face emoji and a blue heart. My phone vibrates a few minutes later with another text. He says he'll call me tonight. Benny has been working his ass off since he was accepted into medical school. Everyone is living their dream. Collecting bridge tolls isn't the most glamorous job in the world, but it will do, for now. My life goals are dependent on Laine and his dreams. It may not be very feminist of me, but I don't have a future unless he is in it. Wherever he goes, I go.

I zip my phone into the pocket of my backpack and head back to my booth. Three more hours on this shift and I can go home, inhale a super chicken burrito, and take a bath. The phone in my booth rings. It's Heather in booth seven.

"Put on 106.1, it's Flashback Friday!" She places the receiver to the radio so I can hear a distorted version of a Pussycat Dolls song.

I hang up on her and slide open my window to take money from a driver in a BMW. The man pulls to a stop and hands me exact change.

"Have a nice day," he says.

I smile and hit the button to raise the barrier. I watch him pull away and wonder where he works. His shirt was crisp and white, and he had on a dark blue tie. If Laine had gone to UC Davis like he wanted, he could've had a nice corporate job. At this point, I wish he was still making sandwiches or waiting for that elusive city job. Any job would be better than the one he's training for now.

It's been eight weeks; four more and he'll be home. We'll be married. Laine's mom offered to help me plan the big day. I'm keeping things minimal. Just Benny as our witness and Laine's parents. My mom is still fighting for her sobriety. She can't make it a week before she's back at it. Unless she cleans up in the next month, I don't plan on telling her I'm marrying Laine. Mom hasn't spoken to me since the night I puked in the sink. I don't know if she's upset that I'm pregnant or happy she's going to be a grandma. You can't tell with her. She drinks either way.

I didn't post the news of my pregnancy or my upcoming nuptials on social media. The people who matter already know. At least, that's the lie I tell myself. I didn't post my news because of Bryn's parents. I ran into them at Walgreens last week. Frances invited me to the house for coffee. I couldn't say no. The house hadn't changed. Bryn's bedroom was just as I left it the morning of her funeral.

If the baby is a girl, I plan to name her Bryn. If the baby is a boy, Benny thinks we're naming it after him. He takes full credit for our relationship and now for our child. He's insane.

I unlock my front door and hear voices in the kitchen. More importantly, I smell pizza. I toss my keys on the dining room table and drop my backpack on the floor.

"Hey, little bird." Benny walks into the dining room. "How was work?" He kisses my cheek and gives me a quick hug.

I'm in the twilight zone. Benny has never been in my house. Never met my mother.

"Your friend Benny brought pizza for dinner," Mom says from the kitchen. "Do you want a slice?"

I ignore her and ask Benny what the hell he's doing here.

"I had a break in between classes, so I thought I'd come home for a couple of days." He winks and ushers me into the kitchen. "Come on; you need to feed the belly."

Benny stays for two hours. He chats with my mom about school and the weather in New York. She seems almost normal. At eight o'clock I offer to walk Benny to his car. He gives my mother a hug goodbye and then takes my hand as we walk out the door. It's the end of summer, but the sky is still light and the air warm.

"What are you doing?"

"What do you mean?"

I hold up my hand and show our interlocked fingers. "What is this?"

His brings my hand to his lips and kisses my knuckles, then lets me go. "I'm sorry. I guess I just missed you. I miss Laine. I don't know."

Being around Benny feels odd. Like it's wrong for me to feel something other than hatred towards him.

"I don't know how to separate my feelings between friendship and more," I explain. "So, when you take my hand, I don't see it as a friendly gesture." I think about the day I took Laine's hand not too far from here. There was

130

nothing innocent about it. I had intentions. Bad ones. Now I feel like Benny is trying to get revenge.

Benny stops walking. "This"—he holds my hand up—"this is just me caring about my best friend's baby mama." He laughs. "Me caring about the first girl I ever loved."

"Don't," I warn and start to pull away.

"At this point, it would be weird to come home and not see you, little bird. You're my best friend by proxy."

We've been texting and talking on the phone for the last two months. Why is seeing Benny face to face any different?

"I got a postcard from Laine. It was at my parents' house. He doesn't have my address in New York." Learning Benny got a postcard pisses me off a little. It means Laine sent a card to everyone, not just me. It's bad enough I didn't get the recruit depot call. Laine told me ahead of time that he was going to call his mom, but it still hurt. At some point, he will have to stop being their son and become my husband.

"I know you can't tell from handwriting, but I think he's doing good, don't you?"

I shrug. "I guess so."

"This sucks for you, but this is what he wants. What he's always wanted." We stop at Benny's Audi.

"I'm happy if Laine is happy." The irony of my statement brings me back to the day I broke up with Benny.

131

I didn't want my happiness to be dependent on his yet I'm happy to oblige Laine. His well-being is my number one priority. It just reinforces the fact that Benny and I didn't belong together. I sort of laugh and Benny looks at me like I'm crazy.

"What's so funny?"

"Nothing." I shrug. "Us."

Benny smiles and gets in the car. He starts the engine, then rolls down the passenger window.

"Get in. I'll drive you back to the house."

"No, I'd rather walk."

Benny leans over the passenger seat. "Is everything okay? I mean, your mom seemed clear-headed."

Laine must have told him about her. That's why he showed up today. I know Laine is concerned for me, but he had no right to tell Benny my family business.

"She's good right now. And if she weren't, I'd still be fine." I walk away from the car and cross the street before he has a chance to reply.

Benny texts me an hour later to apologize. He says he flies out Saturday and expects me to have lunch with him before he goes. I text him back the middle finger and tell him I'm craving Greek food.

HAWK SIGHTING
Chapter Eighteen

Two lanes away, a rusted white van creeps towards the toll booth. The man in the passenger seat looks like Hawk. I call Heather's booth.

Pick up.

"Yeesss," she drawls.

"The dude in the van, the passenger"

"Ew, what about him."

"Ask him if his name is Hawk."

"Hawk?"

"Yes. Hurry before the metering light turns green."

Heather keeps the phone to her ear while she asks the man in the van if his name is Hawk.

"Who the fuck wants to know?" Hawk yells back.

I laugh. "Tell him Alee needs to see him."

"Are you fucking kidding me, Al?"

"Just do it."

Heather relays the message. I can't see or hear his reply because a truck rolls into my lane blocking the view. I press the paid button and wave him through. By the time the truck passes, the white van is headed towards the city.

"Who the hell is that?" Heather returns to the phone. "Please don't tell me you're snaking Laine with that pedo."

"That was my father."

"Get the fuck out of here!" She screams. A woman in the mini-van outside Heather's booth gasps. "We are talking about this later. No not you, ma'am." Heather hangs up.

We share an UBER home and I tell Heather everything there is to know about Hawk.

"You're the first and only person I've told."

"I'm honored?" Heather pats my leg. "Seriously, this is some heavy shit. Why haven't you told Laine?"

I know the answer to her question but I don't give it to her. Some things I want to keep to myself. Sharing Hawk with Laine, or vice versa, makes the situation complicated. Hawk is part of my life that doesn't need to be shared. It's already too much when it's just me and him. Laine wouldn't understand; he would judge. The only person with the right to judge my father is me.

"What about your mom?" Heather smacks my leg. "I bet she would murder him if he showed up at your door."

"Yeah, totally."

MY MARINE
Chapter Nineteen

When you grow up in a house like mine, you're accustomed to the suck. The suck is what you know. When things are good, you expect something to go wrong at any minute. Benny flew home yesterday so we could drive to San Diego together. Eight hours in the car with my ex wasn't as bad as you might imagine. I slept most of the way. Benny has great taste in music and never complained about pulling over eighteen times so I could pee. The drive didn't suck.

Benny checked us into a hotel near the beach. We're supposed to meet Laine's parents in thirty minutes for dinner. They arrived an hour ago and opted for a motel closer to the base.

"You ready to go?" Benny enters my room through the adjoining door.

"Tell them I'm sleeping," I say to Benny as he paces from the door to the window. "I can't do small talk tonight."

"Are you sure you're okay?" He stops and checks his hair in the mirror. "Do you need anything? Should I bring food back for you?" He walks to the bed and sits down. He strokes my leg, and I move it away.

"I'm good. I'll call room service if I get hungry."

"Okay, well, charge it to the room," he insists. He refused to let me pay for my room. I wasn't going to argue. "Call me if you need anything. I'll come right back." He walks to the door and makes a big deal about placing the Do Not Disturb sign on the handle outside.

"Goodnight, Alee."

"Goodnight, Benny."

I watch the sunset from my balcony and wonder what Laine is doing at this very moment. I log the time: 7:28. I'll ask him tomorrow when I see him. The realization of what is happening washes over me. Tomorrow I will see Laine. *My Laine.* I look in the direction of his base. I know it's about twenty minutes north of here. Benny and I entered it into the GPS so we could gauge what time we need to leave in the morning for his graduation.

The cool ocean breeze flows past, and I swear I smell him. The earthy scent of his skin. The sweet smell of his hair. Okay, his hair isn't sweet-smelling. It's my fantasy. If I want to pretend Laine's hair smells like lavender and blueberry, I will. When the sky fades to black, I head inside. I've waited twelve long weeks, what's another twelve hours.

★★★

A soft, continuous knocking pulls me from sleep. I sit up and check the time. It's one-fifteen in the morning. I rub my hand over my belly. It's not quite a baby bump, more like a weekend of carbs and beer. The knocking continues. Then I hear my name.

"Alee," Benny says through the door that connects our rooms.

I get out of bed and walk to the door. I check the knob; it's locked. "Benny, go to sleep."

"I can't." He tries the knob. "Let me in." His voice is thick and sloppy.

"No, go to sleep." I start back to bed when a loud thud hits the door.

My first thought is Benny might have fallen and hit his head. Then I hear sobbing and mumbling. I sit on the floor and listen to the sounds coming from his room. His phone dings with a text. I hear him shuffle to pick it up, then swearing.

"Fucking bitch," he sneers and mumbles to himself about his life, his choices. He gets two more texts and tells his phone to fuck off.

I return to bed with my eyes fixed on the ceiling. He's hurting or scared. I hear it in his voice. As his friend, I want to open the door; I want to comfort him. As his ex, I just want to go to sleep. I want tomorrow to come quickly so I can see Laine.

There is another reason I don't open the door. It has nothing to do with Laine. It's the same reason I don't want to hold Benny's hand or let him touch my leg. His emotional state scares me. I'm afraid that opening the door will mean something to him. I don't want to blur any lines. Not now. Not ever.

***

My alarm goes off and I jump out of bed. I wake earlier than this for work, but I didn't sleep well. I take a shower, dry my hair, and then twist it into a bun. I'll take it down before we leave, so my hair will have a nice, natural wave. Just the way Laine likes it. Pregnancy has done amazing things to my body. I can't wait to show it off to Laine.

I'm zipping up my boots when I get a text. I walk to the phone, feeling hopeful that it may be Laine. It's Kelly. She's asking what time I'll be at the base. I tell her nine and she sends back a thumbs-up emoji. I put my phone down and another text comes in. It's from Janey. They're having breakfast at a nearby diner and would like me to join them. I feel bad for flaking on dinner last night, so I tell her I'll be there in fifteen minutes. Then I remember my only ride is Benny.

I gently knock on the door between our rooms.

"Benny, you up?"

The door clicks, and I feel the knob move in my hand. "Let me in." His voice is softer than it was last night.

The daylight seems to make it safe to open the door.

"Morning, little bird." He steps into my room, already showered and dressed. "Do you have any Tylenol?" He walks to the table where a bottle of water sits. He finishes it off. "Ah, man. I needed that." He tosses the bottle in the trash. "I ended up at a bar after dinner, and I did a few too many shots." Of course he's going to blame it on the alcohol.

"I don't have any pain meds. It's a no-no when you're pregnant," I remind him.

"Right." He nods. "So, you want to get some breakfast? You gotta feed the belly."

"Yeah, Laine's parents want us to meet them at the diner."

"All right, let's roll." He heads to his room to get his phone.

I close the door between our rooms and lock it, though I won't need to worry about drunk Benny knocking on my door tonight because I'll be in here with Laine.

Janey and James are sipping coffee at a corner booth when we arrive. A group of Laine's cousins are seated at a table nearby. They stand and greet us. There are a lot of military families here. They have the same nervous look about them.

"Good morning, Alee." Janey stands and hugs me. "You're starting to get a little bump." She gestures to the lump above my waist.

"I think it's more donuts and ice cream than baby," I admit.

"Morning, Alee." James waves from his seat and I wave back.

Benny sits beside me, with his arm across the back of the booth. James takes note of his comfortable demeanor, and I move farther down the bench until I'm up against the wall.

"How was your night?" James asks. "I'm sorry you didn't make it to dinner. Everything okay?"

"Yeah, I was just tired," I tell him as I scan the menu.

"Don't worry, sir." Benny pats my shoulder. "I made sure she had everything she needed."

I give Benny a *WTH* look. He smiles like he's in control. Of me.

We eat and make small talk about Laine. What he looks like in his uniform. How much weight he's gained or lost.

The waitress stops at the table and asks if we want more coffee.

"No, just the check," James tells her. She sets it on the end of the table.

"I got this." Benny reaches for the check, but James snatches it before Benny can grab it.

"No, I got this," he says with a stern look. "Alee, do you want to use the bathroom before we head out?"

Benny begrudgingly exits the booth so I can get out.

James walks behind me to the bathroom and stops at the cashier. I don't take long in the restroom. When I finish, he's waiting outside the door.

"Is everything okay?" He looks back at the table where Benny is texting on his phone. "Is Benny bothering you in any way?" Having Laine's father ask me this is jarring.

"No, of course not." A sense of guilt immerges even though nothing has happened between Benny and me. I've made sure of that.

James sort of holds his hands up like he's not trying to pry. "I just had to ask."

I don't ask him why. I know why. We just leave it at that and head to the car.

Laine's parents are invited to join a parents' support group gathering. Benny and I wait with the other friends and extended family in a courtyard. I'm pacing nervously when I see Kelly through the crowd.

"Alee!" she yells, then quickly ducks her head when a guard turns her way. "Damn, forgot where I was." I hug her, and that's when she notices my belly. "Oh my gosh! You're having a boot camp baby!" She rubs my tiny bump with both hands. "Don't tell me you're going to get married during the ten-day leave."

I cringe and tell her we are. "Is that bad?"

"I'm no better. I made him marry me before boot." She holds her hand up to show off her wedding band like I haven't already seen it on Facebook. "I'll help you with all the paperwork and DEERS bullshit."

I have no clue what she's talking about, but I appreciate her offer. If Laine and Liam are assigned to the same base, it'll be nice to have a friend.

A few more people arrive, and at exactly eight-thirty they tell us we can head to the parade deck. I sit between Laine's parents; his cousins take up half a row below us. Benny sits with them. When Laine's platoon is called, Janey squeezes my hand. She tells me she sees him; I can't tell him apart from the others. His father has tears in his eyes the entire time. I wonder if he feels responsible for this. Laine wouldn't have enlisted if the city job had come through or if he had gone to UC Davis. James catches me watching him and puts his arm around my shoulder. For the first time in a long time, I feel loved. Wanted. Understood.

When the ceremony is over, it's a madhouse. We weave through a crowd of khaki shirts and blue pants searching for Laine. I see Liam first. He hugs me tight, then asks if I've seen Kelly. I point him in her direction and he takes off running. Then I hear the sound of grown men screaming in joy. It's Laine's cousins; they found him. I watch from a safe distance as they assault each other with hugs and slaps on the back. When he reunites with Benny, it brings tears to my eyes. His parents are next; he gives each one a long, silent greeting. I wave to him, nervously from behind his father. James steps aside. Laine's eyes drift over my face, down my torso, and land on my belly. He drops to his knees and kisses the little bump. His mother bursts into tears. Then he lifts me in the air and spins me around.

"I wouldn't do that if I were you."

"I don't care if you puke all over me; I'm so fucking happy to see you." His mouth crushes mine. My bottom lip throbs from the force of him, and my body erupts in pleasure. I can't wait until I have him alone. "I missed you so much, Alee." He presses my body against him. "Oh God, you feel so good," he whispers in my ear.

After Laine is released and ready to go, he tells Benny he wants to drive home immediately.

"But I got the rooms for one more night. We can hang down here then drive back tomorrow." Benny starts to rattle off the plans he's made, but Laine stops him.

"I just want to go home." Laine looks down at me in his arms. They're so much bulkier than when he left. Laine is chiseled and hard. He looks like a modern-day gladiator.

Benny hides his disappointment and we head back to the hotel and check out.

***

We get home around eight at night. Laine's parents decided to stay the extra night in San Diego. I think they did it to give us the house to ourselves. For that, I will be eternally grateful.

Laine takes a shower to wash the Marines off of him and I make us fried egg sandwiches. Our favorite post-sex meal. I place the sandwiches on the desk and hit play on the iPod. The door opens, and my marine walks in with a towel around his waist. We've both changed so much in the last twelve weeks. He rubs his hand over my belly. *Our baby.*

We kiss one long, slow kiss as he pushes against me. For the first time in my life, I understand what the term making love means. His iPod plays on a loop as we laugh, cry, and climax through the night.

I wake in the morning feeling as if nothing can ruin our high. I shower, then get back in bed. We didn't go to sleep until four in the morning, so I decide to let Laine sleep a few more hours. We have an appointment to get our marriage license at two. We're getting married at three forty-five. By tonight, Laine will be my husband.

"Laine," James calls from the hall. He knocks then tries the knob. "Alee, are you awake, sweetie?"

"Yeah." My voice cracks. I get up and unlock the door. I'm wearing one of Laine's USMC t-shirts and a pair of sweats.

He motions for me to come out of the room and then leads me to the kitchen. All of Laine's family business is handled in their kitchen. When I arrive, his mother is crying softly at the table. It hasn't even been twenty-four hours of good. *What could possibly be wrong already?*

"Mike Calderon had a heart attack last night. He didn't make it," James says softly.

I lean against the wall for support as a bolt of lightning strikes my cloud and I come crashing down to earth. I swallow hard and think of Miguel/Mike. He was a prick to me, but he meant a lot to Laine. *Oh God, Benny.* He must be wrecked. He'll need Laine.

"I'll go wake him." I cry in the hall before I wake Laine. Not just for Miguel/Mike. I'm crying for Benny's loss. For the pain that Laine will share with his best friend. And for the wedding I will not be having today.

145

THAT'S WHAT FRIENDS ARE FOR

Chapter Twenty

I convince Laine to go to Benny's alone. I'm the last person Beverly wants to see.

"We're still getting married," he promises.

Today is Friday. They only perform ceremonies on weekdays. Now we have to wait until Monday to get married. It's just three days, then he's mine for the rest of my life.

"You need to be with Benny right now." I kiss him. "Don't worry about me. I'm not going anywhere."

Laine spends all day at Benny's house. Janey volunteers to help contact family members. I show her how to post on Facebook. They decide to have the funeral next Saturday, two days before Laine leaves for infantry training. We still have a lot of time. We'll have to get another witness; Benny is in no shape to stand in a room and watch us get married. I consider calling Kelly or maybe Heather from work. I feel like a dick every time I think about how Miguel/Mike's death is screwing up my plans.

On Monday, Laine promises to help Benny pick out a casket for his father; we don't get married. Laine's training is evident in his demeanor, how he deals with Benny and Beverly. Laine takes control; he's the problem solver. He's strong when they can't be. He earns a new level of respect from me, from everyone.

On Tuesday he escorts Benny and Beverly to meet with their family priest, then he drives them to the cemetery to pick out a burial plot. Our nuptials are put off one more day. Wednesday, Benny gets drunk and Laine stays with him all night to make sure he doesn't hurt himself.

Today is Thursday. I wake up in Laine's bed without him. He's still babysitting Benny. I shouldn't say that. He's caring for his friend. I'm just being selfish. Every day that passes is another missed opportunity for us to be married. It hurts. Actually, my side hurts. My back hurts. I feel nauseated. I gorged at Benny's house last night. They have a steady stream of people stopping by with casseroles and snacks.

I decide to go for a walk to burn some of the unneeded calories. I end up at the bakery where I used to work. I pick up a loaf of ciabatta bread for old times' sake. As I head back up the hill, a sharp pain rips through my abdomen, and I have to stop and catch my breath. A few short quick breaths and I'm able to continue walking.

What did I eat today? What didn't I eat today? I'm on Laine's level when it comes to stress eating. A chocolate donut, two eggs over easy with bacon, and a yogurt. That was before noon. I make it back to Laine's house feeling wiped out and vowing not to have a big dinner. That's until I remember Janey is making lasagna. I pop in to say hi and let her know I stopped by the bakery. "It smells delicious in here." I set the bread on the counter."

"You didn't have to do that, sweetie, but thank you." Janey turns around with a tray in her hands and nearly drops it. "Alee, what's wrong?" She sets the tray on the counter and pulls a chair out for me to sit down. "Are you feeling okay?"

"I didn't sleep well and I overate last night." I think about the spreadable cheese and crackers I inhaled at Benny's house and I feel queasy. "I'll be fine." She hands me a glass of water and tells me to go lie down. I don't argue.

When I wake from my nap, it's dark outside. I hear voices from down the hall. One of them is Laine. His father is telling him it's not good for him to stress this much before infantry training.

"You have to go in with a clear head, son."

"I know, Dad. But what do you want me to do? I can't abandon my best friend right now. He needs me."

"Alee needs you." I'm shocked James is on my side, but it makes me smile.

I stand up to go to the bathroom and feel something sticky and wet between my legs. I pull my jeans down, and the sight of the blood makes my knees weak.

No. No. Oh God, please, no.

I unravel the toilet paper around my hand until it's as fat as a boxer's glove, then I shove it into my pants and pull them up. I don't know why I think this will stop the blood. I just want to pretend I didn't see it. It isn't real. This isn't happening.

"Alee, are you hungry?" Laine's mom walks in, and I realize I didn't shut the bathroom door. She looks inside and sees the blood on the toilet seat.

"I'm sorry," I tell her. *I'm sorry* is all I can think to say.

She steps into the bathroom and closes the door. She pulls me into her arms and we quietly cry together.

"What do I tell him?"

"Nothing." She swallows her grief. "He has too much stress already. His ten-day leave is supposed to be relaxing. He can't go back with this on his mind."

I don't want to tell him. To disappoint him. But how can I lie? He will never forgive me.

"You can write to him later, a month from now. After he's settled. We'll tell him these things happen."

"Okay." I repeat "okay" a few more times. Until it feels right.

She tells me to take a shower while she changes Laine's sheets. When I get out of the shower, a pair of leggings and a few pads wait for me on the counter.

After I shower, I find Laine laying on his bed.

"Hey, baby. I'm so sorry." He folds his arms around me. I grind my teeth together to keep from crying. "I want nothing more than to marry you, but…"

"Don't worry about that right now. I don't need a piece of paper to tell me I'm yours. My heart belongs to you, always." I let a single tear slip down my cheek.

Laine kisses me softly and sits on the bed. His hands move up the back of my thighs, and I worry he'll feel the pad. I step back towards the bathroom.

"I'll be right back." I turn on the bathroom light and close the door. Tears are already falling as I turn the faucet on. The running water cannot mask my sobs. Laine opens the door and takes me in his arms.

"Don't cry, baby." He lifts me so I'm sitting on the edge of the sink.

I remember the day we had sex on this counter. It was a good day. All of my good memories contain Laine. He gave me something to live for after Bryn. He gave me his heart. The tragedy we faced this week isn't the beginning of the end. Hell, it isn't even the worst to come. It's just a plot twist in the story of our lives. I can't wait to write the next chapter. A better chapter.

"You're right, we are more than a legal document and a ring on this finger." He holds my ring finger, then kisses it. "But I'm still going to marry you, Alee Finch."

"Will I keep my name?" I ask and slow my tears.

"If you want or I can be Laine Finch or Laine Dicaro-Finch."

I break into a smile. A genuine smile.

"I want to be Alee Dicaro."

Laine presses between my legs and kisses me. "Then that is who you are. From this moment on. Alee Dicaro."

When Laine tries to carry me to bed, I stop him. I tell him I want to check on my mother.

"I've been gone all week. I should at least make sure she's still breathing."

He doesn't argue. He doesn't protest until I insist on walking home. Luckily, Janey remembers she has to pick up something from the grocery store and offers to drive me.

It's difficult to kiss Laine goodnight. Our days are numbered and leaving him feels wrong. I don't want to put any more strain on him this week. There is no way I can keep a smile on my face when I'm losing our baby.

Janey takes me to Saint Luke's Hospital. They draw my blood to confirm what I already know. A very friendly nurse tells me to come back if I soak more than one pad an hour and to call my doctor next week to make an appointment. Then Janey drives me home. I bleed through the night, silently crying as I fold the pads and shove them in the trash beside my toilet. Every time I stand up to flush, I keep my eyes on the wall. I don't want to see what is being washed away.

I wake up Friday to a text from Laine. He was asked to pick up family from the airport. While plays taxi for the Calderon family, I lay in bed all day. Those fluffy numbered sheep stare down mockingly as tears stream down my temples into my ears. I let them pool there, dampening my hair. My belly feels soft, empty. Once my tears dry, and the bleeding stops, there will be no trace of what almost was. Do people move on as if it never happened? I don't want to forget that part of Laine was growing inside of me. At the hospital, the doctor patted my shoulder, said I was young. Insinuating, I'll have more chances to accidentally get knocked up. This was a gift, not a mistake.

Saturday morning, I wake to the sound of vacuuming. I check the time. I'm late for the funeral. I decide to skip the service at St. Kevin's and the trip to the cemetery. I text Laine and tell him I will meet him at the reception. It's being held at Miguel/Mike's favorite restaurant, a family-owned Greek place in West Portal that Beverly rented for the day.

I'm greeted at the door by the smell of cooked meat and spices. Soft pockets of conversation fill the room. The overhead speakers are playing a Santana song. Miguel/Mike loved Santana. There are at least one hundred people here. None of them know I'm no longer pregnant. The only person who knows is rearranging trays on the long buffet table against the wall.

"Hi, Janey."

She stops fidgeting with a tray of olives long enough to reprimand me for being here. "You should be home resting."

"I had to come."

She scans the room for the boys. "They seemed to have disappeared." She waves it off in that boys will be boys kind of way then returns to rearranging of the buffet. A waiter stands to the side looking annoyed. Micromanaging is how Janey deals with grief.

I wonder if anyone here is really upset Miguel/Mike is gone. How much did he impact the lives of these people? Other than his immediate family, most of the guests are only here for the free food and wine. They'll share stories about Miguel/Mike, eat, drink, then return to their lives as if this day never happened. There are only three people who would attend my funeral. I'll take three people who care about me over a room full of assholes any day.

I don't have any Miguel/Mike stories to share so I eat, drink, then decide to leave. It's been an hour and still no Laine. I find Janey and tell her I'm heading home. She says she'll let the boys know I was here. As I'm walking out, Benny is walking in. He falls onto my shoulder. I struggle to support his weight, suddenly he finds the strength to hold me. He clings to my body and moans my name.

"I'm sorry about your dad." I try to step back, Benny holds on tighter. It's a desperate, angry hug. Like he's trying to squeeze something out of me.

"I fucking love you," he slurs and the familiar stench of bourbon makes me gag. "I love you, little bird."

Laine appears from the street, he grabs the back of Benny's shirt and tosses him. Benny slams against the wall and slides down to the floor.

"Are you okay, Alee? Did he hurt you?" Laine's hand swipes over my belly and I freeze like he will feel there is nothing growing inside me. He kisses my cheek and tells me to go home. That he will come over later.

Before I leave, I watch Laine carry Benny into the restaurant and deposit him into a chair. He gave up his entire ten-day leave to help Benny. Not many friends would do that. Only my Laine.

Laine texts me around nine to say he's on his way. I sit in the front window and wait for him. I stare at my reflection and think of my mother. She sat in this window for weeks, then months, then years, waiting for my father to come home. Now, here I sit. Waiting for the man I love to walk around the corner. *Are we really that different?* I share this commonality with my mother, but the men we love are nothing alike.

Laine's broad physique rounds the corner. His stride is strong; he walks with purpose. I wonder how many miles he's logged in boot camp. I wonder how many miles he still has ahead of him in infantry training. He should be relaxing, enjoying his time home before he starts his sixty days of hell. I open the door before he has a chance to knock. His face lights up when he sees me wearing his USMC t-shirt. He scoops me into his arms and carries me to bed. My heart is in my throat. We can't have sex and I can't tell him why.

The bleeding has slowed, but sex is off-limits for at least six weeks. He sets me gently on the bed, and I tell him my mom is home. That's code for no banging. Once we're married and have our own place, times like this will be a thing of the past. I always imagined, when I dared to imagine, that we would live in a funky apartment in the mission or an overpriced place downtown. I never dreamt we'd move away. The idea of a new town, hell, a new country, will get me through the loneliness of the next two months. Now if could just figure out how I'm going to stomach the next two days.

UNOFFICIALLY MINE

Chapter Twenty One

"Where are we going?" I plead for Laine to tell me why we're on the train this early on a Sunday morning.

"You didn't find God in boot camp did you?"

"There is no God in boot camp, it's pure hell."

"Then where are we going?"

The only things open downtown at this hour are restaurants. My stomach growls at the thought of a fancy brunch. French toast and thick bacon sound heavenly right now.

"It's a secret." He kisses my forehead.

We get off at the Civic Center Station, my heart races as the escalator carries us to the street. I look at the domed building on the other side of the plaza. "Laine, City Hall is closed. They don't perform weddings on Sunday."

The morning sweep has just ended. Police usher the homeless from the area to make room for the Farmer's Market. We continue past the vendors, to the middle of the plaza. A forgotten sleeping bag is draped over the back of a bench and I feel bad for whoever lost it.

"They might be closed, but I made a promise that I intend to keep." Laine kneels down and pulls a box from the pocket of his jacket. "I want to do this right." Laine lets out a long sigh and squints against the morning sun. I step to the side so my body casts a shadow over his sweet face. How ironic that Laine is kneeling in my shadow.

"There is no name or cliché to explain what we have. It is something we built. It is ours and ours alone. This isn't just about want or desire." He opens the box and removes a sapphire ring. "I was made for you." He slides the ring onto my shaky finger, then kisses the oval-shaped sapphire encircled with small diamonds. "I will always be yours." He stands and a crowd applauds. I leap into his arms and we kiss. And we kiss. And we kiss. When I open my eyes, the crowd is gone. I pull away and wipe the tears from my face.

This is the kind of love that changes you. The kind that breaks you down, makes you weak. In Laine's arms, I feel safe. He's my protector, my hero. He is the love of my life.

"I love you, Alee." He rubs my belly. "Both of you."

Hot tears roll down my cheek. I can't keep this from him a second longer. He deserves to know. I selfishly want to tell him. I want to grieve with him. We're stronger together.

"Laine, I need to…." I'm about to tell Laine about the baby when a woman interrupts.

"Excuse me, hi. I saw you get down on your knee, and I just started shooting. I apologize for intruding on your moment, but I thought you wouldn't mind a few pictures."

"No, that's very thoughtful," Laine tells her.

"Here's my card. Email me your mailing address and I'll send you some of the shots." She holds out a card that reads RW Photography.

"She'll have to do it. I report back to base tomorrow."

"Well, in that case, I'll send you all the shots, at no charge." She thanks Laine for his service and walks away. I put the card in the back pocket of my jeans.

"Let's get out of here, I'm starving. I just want to stuff my face and relax today. No more drama." Laine puts his arm around me and turns towards the BART station. "Wait, did you want to tell me something?" He thinks I want to profess my feelings; he has no idea I was about to break his heart.

"I don't remember," I shrug.

Laine laughs. "You're lying, Alee. But that's okay. I know you love me." He kisses my forehead, and we head back to the train.

We have dinner with Laine's parents and then we go to Greenberg's for a drink. I really want a beer, but I have to keep up appearances. We plan to stay an hour but end up hanging out until midnight. By the time we get back to Laine's house, I'm exhausted. Laine thinks it's due to the baby and doesn't try to initiate sex. The whiskey shots he took with his friends help him fall straight to sleep. I stay awake and memorize every detail of his face. He looks so peaceful, so happy. Good. Because he'll be in a living hell for the next sixty days. He doesn't know what kind of free time he'll have or if he can call me. My phone will be glued to my hand every minute he's gone.

***

Laine wakes at nine. He jokes about it being the last time he'll sleep in for a while. His mother makes him a huge breakfast, which includes steak and mashed potatoes. We share our last hours together with his parents and cousins. We were supposed to drive back to San Diego with Benny. That isn't happening now. Laine got a flight out of SFO at noon. I don't want to share my goodbye with his family. I want to see him off alone, just the two of us. His cousins insist on tagging along. We pile into his father's SUV and

160

drive to the airport. They rap/sing with the songs on the radio, it brings much-needed levity to the journey.

Our group is a spectacle as we stand in front of the security checkpoint to say goodbye. People notice Laine is dressed in jeans and a USMC t-shirt and understand the reason for the big send off. Laine slings his duffel bag over his shoulder, and I can't help but think of my father. Laine is the only man I have ever loved, the only man who has ever loved me. Even though he won't be in any real danger, I am scared to death of losing him. He says his goodbyes to his family then pulls me aside.

"I'm sorry things didn't work out the way we planned. When I come back, nothing is going to stop me from marrying you. We'll go to Vegas or Tahoe," he promises.

I nod my head and kiss his cheek. He turns his head so our lips touch. It's the last kiss we'll share for a long time. Without warning, he places his hand on my abdomen. I look at his mother. It kills me when he presses his lips to my empty belly and whispers, "I love you." The tears I was holding back come in waves. I heave and cry. Laine tries to console me, but I can't stop. His mother finally walks over. She takes Laine's hand and explains what happened.

"You lost the baby?" His words are not meant to be hurtful, but they feel like a knife in my chest. *I lost the baby*.

Me. Alee. I did it. I fucked up and let that little life slip through my fingers. I lost Laine's baby.

Janey rubs my back and says, "These things happen. It's nobody's fault. Alee was put through a lot of stress this week." They hug and she whispers something in his ear; he nods. "I love you, son." She kisses his cheek and retreats to the group.

"I'm sorry, I wanted to tell you, but I—"

"Shh, I know." He pulls me into his arms and rubs my back. "This doesn't change anything. I love you, Alee." He releases me and walks away.

He turns around one last time as he passes through security and waves to us. Then he's gone.

YO!

Chapter Twenty Two

I sit on the concrete wall with an iced coffee and a bag of chips. I eat one, then toss one to the birds. It's a warm day, the street is alive with shoppers. Young girls looking for good deals on cheap clothes. Couples holding hands, window shopping wedding dresses at Diana's. Hipsters sipping eight dollar coffees inside a newly opened café while the homeless panhandle outside.

"Yo! Alee!" I hear Hawk's voice but I don't see him.

A frightened hipster and her hipster dog scamper past the wall as Hawk runs up behind them. Even from fifty feet away I can tell he's high. His eyes are dilated past human, lips dry and cracked.

"Hey, Hawk." Reginald comes around the corner and intercepts him. His cart blocks the sidewalk forcing hipsters into the street to avoid his homelessness. "Pink Floyd is looking for ya." Pink Floyd is a local gangster, drug dealer, car thief. Hawk does *work* for him now and then.

Hawk looks around, terrified. "Which way did he go?" He grabs at his waist and pulls up his pants, ready to run. He looks fifteen pounds lighter than the last time I saw him.

"That way." Reginald points and Hawk runs off in the opposite direction. Reginald pushes his cart to the wall and sits beside me. "He'll be pissed I lied, but he'll thank me when he's sober. He doesn't want you to see him like that."

"How do you know?"

"'Cause I wouldn't want you to see me if I was whacked out of my mind and you're not even my kid."

"That's the first time I've seen him in months." Not since the van on the bridge. "Where's he been?"

"Sometimes you have to go through it to get over it." Reginald adjusts the bags on the side of his cart. He has more than usual. It's close to the holidays, people are generous this time of year. "I thought you only came around here on Thursday?"

"I like to mix it up." I toss the birds another chip. I offer Reginald the bag. He waves them away.

"Me too. When you stay in one place too long people start to think they know you." He ambles back to his cart. "See you Thursday, Alee."

"See ya, Reg."

I have shared DNA with Hawk. We shoot the shit over fast food, but I don't know him and he doesn't know me. Coming here, to the wall, hoping to run into a man who could care less about my existence, is my addiction.

SEX ON THE BEACH

Chapter Twenty Three

Laine and I talk once a week, except when he's in the field. SOI (School of Infantry) is brutal, but he stays focused on the end game: graduation and marrying me. He has access to a computer, so he emails whenever he can. I keep my messages light and positive. I don't burden him with my issues; they don't matter. Nobody is shooting a gun at me for fun. Dealing with the occasional prick on the bridge or missing my train home is nothing compared to what Laine will face when he gets his orders.

I lurk in the military friends and family support groups on Facebook. Reading their comments makes me feel less alone. The consensus is that Laine will go to Afghanistan. One of the fathers in the group is some kind of conspiracy theorist. He watches all the news sources. He said they're holding elections in Afghanistan and our troops will offer support.

If Laine deploys, I won't see him until he returns, which will most likely be a year from now. I can't go a year without him. I can't go another week. His graduation is in four days. He gets two days off for Thanksgiving. His parents rented a beach house in San Diego so he won't have to waste any time traveling to see us. From the pictures Janey showed me the house is huge. Hopefully, our bedroom is far from theirs.

I pull my phone from my locker and check for new messages. Nothing from Laine or Benny. I haven't spoken to Benny since his father's funeral. I texted him once or twice to say hi and he never wrote back. I try not to read into it. He's busy. I'm insignificant. Whatever. I'm about to put my phone away when it rings. I don't even get a chance to say hi before Janey's voice explodes through the phone.

"Laine called!" She waits half a beat before continuing. At this point, I don't care that he called his mother and not me. I'm just elated he made it through SOI. "He figured you might be at work and didn't want to risk calling and you not answering."

"It's fine. What did he say?"

"He's excited to see us and he wanted to make sure I was making my baked macaroni and cheese." She rambles about how it's his favorite food. "He wanted to let us know that after dismissal, he only has a forty-eight-hour leave. I told him the house was nearby, so he didn't have to worry about travel time."

"Is that all?" I ask. I realize she might take it the wrong way. "I mean; did he ask for anything else he might need or want us to bring?"

"No, sweetie, he just wanted to make sure we were going to be there and to say hi."

I tell her I'm happy he called her, then we hang up. I'm excited to see him, but I'm also scared. I don't know who he is going to be. Will this version of Laine still love me? During our correspondence, he never talked about the baby. There is nothing to discuss.

***

I'm packed and waiting for Laine's parents to pick me up. We're leaving a day early to get everything in order before Laine's graduation. Nobody wants to waste a single second of our time with him.

"Alee," Mom calls from the hall.

"Yeah," I yell. "I'm in my room."

The door opens and my mom's face peeks in. "How do you feel about having a turkey breast this year? I found this recipe online. I brine the breast overnight; it's supposed to make it really juicy."

Crap. Did I forget to tell her I wasn't going to be home for Thanksgiving? She's been sober since Laine left for SOI. She's always sober before the holidays. She usually waits until the kitchen is full of dishes and dirty pots to escape into her bottle, leaving me to clean up the mess.

"I'm not going to be here." I pretend to check my overnight bag to avoid looking at her. I shouldn't feel bad. I shouldn't even care. She's left me alone more times than I can count.

"Oh," she says. "Did Laine's parents invite—"

"No," I interrupt her. "Laine is graduating from SOI." I don't explain the acronym to her; it doesn't matter. "He gets two days leave before he's deployed. I'm going to spend the weekend with him in San Diego."

I don't tell her his parents are joining us. If she knew, it would hurt her, and even though she deserves it, I don't want to twist the knife. You know, karma and all that.

"Oh, I understand." She backs out of my room and closes the door.

A few minutes later I hear the front door open and close. It doesn't take a genius to know she is going to drink the moment I leave the house. For all I know, this is good news. She can drink in peace.

***

The drive to San Diego isn't as long this time. I don't have to stop every forty minutes to pee. We get to the house just as the sun is setting. Laine's parents drop me off then go to the grocery store. I'm unpacking when my phone buzzes. I jump over the bed and snatch it from the nightstand. I accidentally pull the charger out of the wall, and it falls onto the hardwood floor with a loud thud. It's a text from Benny saying he's outside and to open the door. *Can't he ring the doorbell like a normal person?*

I roll over the squeaky bed and land on the other side. I put my phone in the back pocket of my jeans as I open the bedroom door. Then I scream.

Benny is standing in the hall outside my room.

"You fucking asshole!" I punch his arm, his chest, his arm again.

"Sorry, little bird." He laughs as if my assault is funny. "With all that squeaking it sounded like you were doing something naughty in here." He steps around me into the room and hops on the bed.

I remain in the doorway. "What are you doing?"

"Just checking out the bed." He winks and puts his hands under his head. "Pretty comfy."

"Well, your room is down there." I point down the hall assuming he has a room. "So I suggest you go get comfy on your own bed."

"Come on, Alee." He sits up. "It isn't like we haven't shared a bed before." He plucks a t-shirt out of my bag and smells it.

"Don't be weird." I snatch the shirt and move the bag to the other side of the room. I set it on the dresser and steady my breathing. The unease I felt the last time I was with Benny resurfaces.

Benny walks to the window. He moves the curtains to the side and stares towards the beach. The sky has a faint blue tone as if it refuses to relent to the night. I stand behind Benny and watch the stars fall into place. There is something magical about watching the sky turn to night over the ocean.

"Do you ever think about us?" He speaks softly, as if he doesn't want to disturb the show outside. His face is lit by the small lamp beside the bed and I see the broken boy from the side yard at school. *How could I ever be afraid of him? It's just Benny.*

"What do you mean?"

"I mean do you ever think about *us.* Our time together. Sometimes I think about when I was the one loving you."

Oh no. He's going there. He's really going there. And now I have to lie. "Only when I hear that Sean Kingston song."

Benny smiles. "That was our theme song."

"Yeah, it was." I walk towards the door. "Come on, I'll show you where you're sleeping." I have no clue what the room assignments are, I just want him out of mine.

Benny grabs my hand and pulls me back. "Wait." The forcefulness in the way he holds me causes my defenses to go up.

"Don't." The fierce look on my face is enough warning for him to let me go.

I tell Benny his room is at the end of the hall, and he walks out. When I hear the shower turn on, I exhale. *Is this my fault? Do I lead him on in some way?* I wonder if I'm overreacting, reading too much into this. Benny was having a vulnerable moment, and I treated him like a stranger assaulting me on the street. He's right, we do have history, but we were just kids. I turned seventeen two months after we started dating. Our youth doesn't discredit what we shared—Benny and I were in love. We shared intimate moments with each other that, at the time, felt very real. The kisses, the hugs, the other stuff, too. Benny and I had a lot of sex. Sometimes we did it three times a day. His house, his car, at school. Kids like to fuck. Laine and I transcend the physical. Our connection is spiritual. Nothing will break us apart. Not time, or distance, or the fucking United States Marine Corps.

172

When Laine's parents return, I help them unload the groceries. A few minutes later, Benny walks into the kitchen shirtless. His hair is still wet from his shower.

"Benny, I didn't know you were here." Janey shuts the refrigerator and gives him a hug.

James takes notice of me in my sweatpants and a tank top, then looks at Benny's freshly showered, half-naked body. His eyes turn cold. I feel like I need to explain.

"Sorry, Benny got in like half an hour ago." It was more like an hour but I don't want Laine's father to think we were alone the entire time they were out shopping. "He went to take a shower and I totally forgot he was here. Out of sight, out of mind."

Janey laughs and hands her husband a box of breadcrumbs to put into the cabinet above his head. "You have Laine on the brain." She laughs. "We all do."

Benny watches me from the doorway with a smug look on his face. I throw an apple at his head, he catches it and takes a bite. He thinks I felt some sort of way when we were alone, a way Laine's parents wouldn't approve of. He's wrong, but he's also right.

James grills burgers for dinner. Janey makes potato salad. She saves a healthy portion of it and a burger for Laine to eat tomorrow. Apparently, Laine loves his mother's potato salad. After dinner, Janey goes to the kitchen to start chopping things for the stuffing she will make on Thanksgiving. I offer to help, but she won't let me. She suggests Benny and I take a walk. James looks like he wants to strangle her. Benny jumps at the idea, and we head to the beach.

"Do you think they want us out of the house so they can have sex?" Benny nudges my arm with his elbow.

"That's gross." I try to wipe the visual from my mind. "Just in case, let's give them an hour."

The beach turns out to be a little too windy, so we end up at a dive bar. I make Benny promise we'll only stay an hour. We pinky promise. Benny orders sex on the beach, just to be ironic. There are only three other people in the place: two guys playing pool and a bored girl on her phone. I want to say something about our conversation earlier, but I'm not sure if a tipsy talk about our relationship is wise. I limit the dialogue to Laine, what he's been through, where he's going. We talk a little about Benny's grades. What his plans are for the future.

"I fully intend to come back to San Francisco to practice. I don't know how many more New York winters I can take. The snow is brutal." He sips the last of his drink. "I guess you don't appreciate how good you have it until it's gone." He winks at me then tells the bartender we want another round.

"Do we have time?" I look for a clock.

"It's only been thirty-five minutes." He points to his wrist. I tell him it's cool that he wears a watch.

"It's a doctor thing. For checking pulses and shit."

"Pulses and shit? Is that the official term?"

"I don't have to be official with you." He rubs the back of my hand with his. "You're my little bird. I've seen you naked."

Here we go again. I retract my hand and shake my head in disapproval. "Benny…"

"Don't freak out, I'm just teasing you." Benny spins on his stool to face me. "Can't we just talk about it? Is that so bad?"

"It feels wrong to talk about us and sex."

"Who said anything about sex?"

"You know what I mean."

"The fact is, we were together before you and Laine. During you and Laine," he jabs. "Eating pizza after my games. Making out in the bathroom at Starbucks. Those were good times. I don't see why we have to pretend they never happened."

I enjoyed being with Benny. Then, one day, I didn't. I can't even blame him. He didn't want to lose me. He might have even tried to change for me. I didn't want a new and improved Benny. I wanted Laine.

"You're right. We don't have to pretend it didn't happen. But sometimes, and hear me out—" I pause and touch his hand. He flips it over so we are palm to palm.

"See, this"—I hold his hand up in the air—"this feels like you want to reenact some of those old memories."

Benny puts down his glass and laughs. He laughs so long I start to laugh.

"What's so funny?"

"You." He leans forward and folds me into his arms. "I fucking love you."

My head falls back in exasperation. "Benny," I scold.

"Alee, I love you. That doesn't mean I want to fuck you. We're friends. We loved each other and now we love Laine, together. In the most un-gay way possible," he clarifies. "I hold your hand the same way I bro-hug Laine. I call you *little bird* with the same affection I call him *dude*."

What he's saying actually makes sense. He sees our situation from an enlightened point of view.

Benny checks his watch. "Time's up, princess." He pulls his wallet out and places forty dollars on the bar. "Drink up."

I suck down the rest of my cocktail and hop off the stool. Benny tells the bartender to have a good night. I loop my arm with Benny's and rest my head on his shoulder. "I'm actually glad we had that conversation."

176

"Me too." He kisses the top of my head and we walk out into the windy San Diego night.

"I feel like we're on the same page now." I point to my eyes, then towards his.

"We're here." Benny agrees.

"Exactly! Totally in sync. Like Avatar level *I see you*, shit."

"No, I mean we're here," Benny points to the house.

"Oh shit, I'm drunk." I make Benny go first. "Do really think they had sex?"

"If I were alone in this house with the woman I love, it'd be so on." He runs his hand down my cheek, then jerks the door open like he's a cop serving a warrant. He raises an eyebrow and announces our arrival in a loud obnoxious tone. "We're baaack."

James stops clicking the remote long enough to ask how the walk was. I notice he's changed into a pair of sweatpants and a t-shirt.

"Windy," Benny says.

I giggle. *Goddamn, sex on the beach.*

James glares at us. Benny sits in the recliner and asks what's on tv. I hope James can't smell the alcohol from where he's sitting. I escape to the kitchen.

"Want some help?" I pick up a stray carrot and eat it. Colorful piles of freezer bags sit on the counter. "Wow, that's a lot of chopping." I inspect a bag of onions.

Janey turns off the water and wipes her hands on a towel. "I'm just about done in here." She opens the refrigerator and carefully places the bags inside by color. "Why don't you get to bed." She looks at the clock, it's past ten. "The sooner you go to sleep, the faster tomorrow comes.

I agree.

STOP ASKING IF I'M OKAY

Chapter Twenty Four

Laine's graduation isn't as grandiose as the one they held after boot. The stands aren't even half full. We wait nearly two hours for Laine to be dismissed. He walks through the gate and drops his duffel bag to hug his dad. His mother is next. Janey finally lets him go, and he looks in my direction. His face is hard, serious.

"Hey, beautiful." He lifts me into his arms with ease. He's stronger and leaner than he was the last time I saw him. "I missed you."

"I missed you more."

He kisses me softly. I taste mouthwash on his breath.

"Damn, dude!" Benny interrupts. "You're a fucking killing machine." I move to the side so Benny and Laine can hug. "How are you, man?"

"I'm good." Laine lets him go. "How are you doing. You holding up?"

Benny nods and tells Laine he's straight.

"Good." Laine regards him for a few seconds, then breaks away and says, "Let's get out of here. I'm starving."

We have lunch at a seafood restaurant on the Strand, then head back to the house. Laine's father pulls into the driveway, and a man wearing the same dress blues as the graduates at the base is sitting on the porch. Laine jumps out to greet him. They shake hands like they haven't seen each other in weeks when it's only been two hours. Nobody in the SUV speaks. I finally slide out and Benny follows.

"Alee, this is Cruz." Laine presents me to his friend. I hold out my hand, and he shakes it gently.

"It's Barret, actually. Barret Cruz."

"Damn, dude. I didn't even know your first name."

"It's all good. It isn't like we need it." The two laugh.

"Cruz is from Florida. He doesn't have time to fly home, and I didn't want him to spend Thanksgiving alone," Laine explains as we walk into the house.

"It's a pleasure to have you." Janey gives me a look then heads to the kitchen to make sure we have enough food. I don't know why she looks so worried; she bought enough to feed his entire platoon.

Benny, Cruz, and James settle into the living room, discussing football. Laine lingers around the sofa before I catch his eye. I nod for him to follow me to our room. Laine places his bag on the dresser. He takes out two perfectly folded shirts and puts them in the top drawer. He unpacks his entire bag without saying a word. I'm lying across the full-size bed when he turns around.

"Come here." I hold my hand out to him.

"I want to change out of these clothes first." He meticulously folds each piece of clothing he removes. I start to match him item for item. I take off my shirt, then my jeans, and toss them on the floor. His eyes glance at the crumpled pile, and he looks as if he's fighting the urge to pick them up.

I kneel on the bed in my underwear and watch him pull his socks off. He stuffs them in his shoes then stands before me in his boxers. "I should shower."

"Like hell you will!" I grab his hand. Laine falls on the bed beside me. I run my hand along the defined lines of his chest and abs. "I can get used to this." I lean in and kiss his neck. He lets out a soft moan. I move my lips from his neck to his ear. He grabs my waist and rolls me on top of him. We kiss. It isn't the same soft Laine kisses. They're hard and purposeful. Angry even.

"Take this off," he says and pulls at my bra straps.

"You take it off," I whisper into his mouth. I cup his face and try to slow his movement as he rips at the clasp of my bra. After his second failed attempt, I reach around and unhook it. Laine tosses it on the floor. "I love you," I say as I hold his face in my hands.

"Yeah, I love you, too." He rushes his words and lunges for my mouth. Before I can object or even take my next breath, he has me on my back. His boxers are off; he's tearing at my underwear.

"Laine. Baby, wait." He doesn't slow. He's yanking my underwear down my leg. "Laine!" I yell. He pulls back, out of breath. "Slow down. We need to get a condom." I point to the nightstand where I've already placed a stash in the drawer.

He falls onto the bed beside me and runs his hand over his face. "I forgot."

I'm not sure if he's saying he forgot that we use condoms for birth control, or that he forgot he needs one at all. Meaning he forgot I'm no longer pregnant.

"You're different."

"I know."

182

We sit quietly, contemplating what this means. Did his training change him? Is he someone new, someone who doesn't love me? Who can't love me? Or was it all we've been through, losing the baby. Maybe it was our time apart that changed his feelings for me.

He sits up and wraps his arms around me.

"My head is a little fucked up. I need time to decompress back into this...us, the real world."

"Okay," I tell him. We can do that.

We lie in bed talking for two hours before Laine kisses me again. When he does, it's the soft, loving kiss I've been longing for. It's my Laine. He slides between my legs and pauses to look at the silver foiled packet sitting on the nightstand.

"I don't want to use it."

"Then don't." I pull gently on his neck so he lowers himself towards me. "I want to feel you."

He kisses me then pulls back. "I never want to use one of those goddamn things again."

Laine makes love to me. We are loud and the bed is noisy and we don't care.

***

It's past six o'clock when we decide to get up. Laine feels bad leaving Cruz with his dad and Benny all day. "Cruz is good people. I need a guy like that watching my back." The mention of Laine deploying makes my stomach hurt.

"Do you know where you're going?"

He nods and puts on a pair of clean boxers.

"Afghanistan."

That crazy dad was right. I pull on a pair of sweats and hold back my tears. When I look up, Laine is watching me.

"I hope you're pregnant." His words freak me out. "I need something real to come back to." He pulls on a USMC t-shirt.

"What do you mean something real?"

"They tell us to stay focused, keep our minds on the job at hand. And I do, for the most part. But I need something else. Something to motivate me to see it through. I need to know I have something back home waiting for me."

"I'm waiting for you."

Laine reaches for my hand. "I'm not saying you'll cheat or leave me, like Kelly left Liam."

This is the first I've heard about Kelly. I make a mental note to unfriend her.

"I might not always have you, but my kid is *my* kid. Nobody can take that away."

I don't know how much emotion I can put into words. Can words even tell him how I feel? Reinforce the fact that

I'm not going anywhere? "Nothing and nobody in this world could ever take me from you."

"Life happens, Alee. If something comes up and we can't be together, I'll always have my child to think of when I'm out there."

I realize what Laine is saying. He needs something to live for. To survive for. Having a child will be the deciding factor for his actions in the field. As committed as we are to each other, he's right. Life does happen. People make mistakes, change. Nothing changes the connection between parent and child. So I've heard.

"If that's the case, then I think we should hedge our bets." I crawl over the bed and kiss the back of his neck.

He turns around and meets my lips.

"Fuck yeah, we should."

***

The next morning Laine is up at dawn. He and Cruz go for a run on the beach. I stumble into the kitchen at seven. Janey is already cooking.

"Can I help?" I ask as I pour coffee into a mug.

"I have it all under control, Alee." She dumps a Ziploc bag of onions, carrots, and celery into a buttered saucepan. It sizzles and steams. "You spend as much time with Laine as you can." She moves the vegetables around with a wooden spoon. "He needs you right now. He needs this."

Does she mean the calm or the sex?

"He needs to have something memorable to carry him through the next year."

I agree.

We had sex four times yesterday. I don't know if I'm ovulating or not. My period has been irregular since the miscarriage. I don't even know if I can get pregnant right now. I consider asking Janey but it feels way too awkward. I take my coffee to the patio, and a few minutes later, Benny joins me.

"You're up early."

He sits in the chair beside mine. "I'm still on New York time." He sips his cup then stretches. "I hit the sack around eight last night, not that you would know."

When Laine and I finally ventured out of our room around eleven, everyone was asleep. Janey left two plates of spaghetti on the stove for us. Laine ate them both.

"Tell me about Cruz. Is he cool?"

"Kind of quiet, like Laine. I can see why they're friends."

"Are you jealous?" I tease and put my bare feet on the side of his chair.

"Of who? Laine or Cruz?"

I roll my eyes and sip my coffee.

"I'm not jealous," Benny says. "I had you first." He sets his mug on the table and grabs my foot. I squeal. I'm very,

very ticklish on my feet. Benny pulls my leg so it's stretched across his lap and continues to run his finger along the bottom of my foot. I kick and scream for him to stop. Suddenly the back door flies open.

Laine, Cruz, and James come running onto the patio. Benny stops tickling me and we freeze, my leg in his lap. Cruz moves first. He taps Laine's shoulder and walks back into the house. Laine follows him.

"Alee, why don't you go take a shower?" James suggests. "The water heater in this house is small. It's going to take a few hours for all of us to get ready."

"Okay," I say and head inside like I was just caught chewing gum in class by the principal. I pass the front door on my way to the bathroom and hear Laine and Cruz on the porch.

"You trust that dude?" Cruz asks Laine.

"I mean, yeah. He's my best friend."

"You were his best friend when you slept with his girl," Cruz reminds him. Laine must have told him all about us. It's only normal when you spend that much time with someone.

"I guess the better question is, do you trust her?" Cruz steps off the porch, drops to the lawn, and starts doing push-ups.

"Count 'em off, soldier!" Laine yells and the conversation ends. I wait a few more minutes to see if he answers the question. After Cruz does one hundred push-ups, Laine takes a turn.

"Damn, he's like a whole new Laine," Benny says over my shoulder. He's so close I smell the coffee on his breath. The last thing I want is for Laine to catch Benny and me spying on him. Especially now that I know he has trust issues.

"I'm gonna hit the shower."

"Alee, hold up." Benny follows me.

I don't want him to follow me. Not because he scares me. I don't want him near me because every other male in this house seems to think it's wrong. For that, I feel bad. He's just being Benny. My friend. Laine's friend. As blurred as things have been between us, I feel like I finally understand him. He made his feelings clear at the bar. I finally feel at ease around him.

"Is it me, or is Laine's dad being super weird?" He leans against the wall outside my room. "It's like he doesn't want us to talk."

I lie and tell him I didn't notice. I pretend everything is copacetic because that's what I do.

"Maybe I'm just being sensitive."

"You are. Why don't you quit being a little bitch and go do some push-ups or something." I push his chest and he moves back slightly.

"Oh, I see, you want to see me all swelled up like those two jarheads out front." Benny moves the sleeve of his t-shirt so his bicep is showing. "You can't handle this." He flexes.

We're laughing innocently when Laine materializes at the end of the hall. We both hold our breath as he walks towards us. Benny turns so his back is to the wall. The hallway feels really small with the three of us standing in it.

"What's up, dude," Benny says. "You want to go for a swim?" It's freezing outside, so I find it very strange that Benny would ask Laine if he wants to jump into the Pacific Ocean at eight in the morning.

"Sure," Laine calls his bluff. He yells some military jargon to Cruz.

"Why the hell do you want to do that?" Cruz moans from the living room. "We're on leave, dude!"

"Report to the front lawn in fifteen minutes, private!" Laine yells back.

I look at Benny and he shrugs. "Give me five minutes to change and go shit my pants," Benny jokes. "Or vice versa."

Benny walks away and I enter our room. Laine remains in the hall, sweaty and looking like he doesn't want to be here.

"Are you okay?" I wrap my arms around his torso.

"Do me a favor, Alee."

"Sure, anything."

"Don't ask me if I'm okay. It's annoying." He taps out of my embrace and walks into the bedroom.

I won't have to ask again. I know he isn't.

After the guys leave for their swim, I shower and get dressed. I put on a pair of red high-waisted skinny jeans and a white tunic. It's long and extends past my waist. I wrap a red and gray plaid scarf around my neck, then slip on a pair of leather boots. I love these boots. They're tan with a strap that buckles across the top, that hits right below my knee. They're the most expensive thing I've ever bought for myself. I dry my hair and put on a little makeup. I want to look good today. For Laine. This is the last day we'll spend together for who knows how long. I want everything to be perfect.

Familiar Thanksgiving smells fill the house. Laine's mother has outdone herself. Janey puts me in charge of making the salad. It's the only thing that doesn't require any skill. I chop lettuce and dice cucumbers while James watches football in the other room. He comes in every fifteen minutes to remind us the guys are still gone. It's been two hours. He's about to go looking for them when the front door opens.

"Something smells really good in here!" Laine yells from the living room. Ten seconds later he walks into the kitchen, dripping wet. "I'm starving!" He picks a cucumber out of my salad and tosses it in his mouth.

"Laine, you're getting water all over the floor!" Janey scolds. "Alee, go get a couple of towels from the hall closet for Aquaman." She throws her hand towel on the floor to soak up the puddle under her son.

I leave to get the towels, and the front door opens again. Cruz and Benny are laughing as they walk into the house. I catch Benny's eye and he whistles.

"Alee, you look stunning." He walks towards me, and I put up my hand to stop him.

"Don't move! You guys are wet and sandy. I'll get you a towel." I grab three towels from the closet and take them back to the living room. I give one to Benny, and one to Cruz.

"Thank you, Alee," Cruz says and wipes his face. "Benny is right, you look beautiful."

"Thank you." I blush.

Laine walks up behind me and takes the towel from my hand. "Will you two jackasses quit flirting with my girl and go take a shower." Laine kisses my cheek. "You first, Calderon."

Benny gives him a salute, then turns on his heels and marches down the hall. Cruz and Laine laugh more at him than with him.

After the boys shower, we finally assemble around the table and James says grace. The boys cross themselves and mumble amen. In all the dinners I've shared with the Dicaro's, that was a first. People tend to find God when it's convenient. Believing in a higher power, something with the ability to protect, even save lives, comes in handy when someone you love is in the face of danger.

Laine, Cruz, and Benny eat a lot. So much that Janey notes they won't have any leftovers to eat tomorrow.

"There is no tomorrow," Laine mumbles through a mouthful of mac and cheese.

My heart falls into my stomach. I see Janey flinch as well. She recovers quickly. "Well, don't forget we still have dessert."

When all of the pies have been sampled and the mashed potatoes are gone, we force Janey to sit on the sofa with a glass of wine so we can do the dishes.

"That was two hours of my life I'll never get back," Benny complains as he places the last plate into the cabinet.

192

Cruz scoffs and says, "Shit, I'll take dish duty over patrol any day of the week." He holds his fist out and Laine bumps it.

"When I'm done with school, these pretty hands are going to save lives," Benny boasts and holds up his wrinkled fingers.

"So will these," Cruz says. He makes a gun with his hand and aims it at Benny, then pulls the trigger. Benny grips his chest and grunts like he was hit. They laugh. They think it's funny.

I don't. "I'm going to bed."

The guys say goodnight, I hear Benny mumble something about it being a good night for Laine, and the boys laugh.

I take off my clothes and slip on the USMC shirt Laine gave me. I crawl into bed when I hear Laine tell his parents goodnight. This is our last night together. Our last opportunity to make a baby. The small desk lamp shines a dim light on Laine when he enters the room. He undresses then slides behind me into bed. He kisses my shoulder and wraps me in his arms. "I miss this more than anything else," he whispers. "I miss holding you."

"This is what I miss." I reach down and stroke him. He moans and rolls on top of me.

He lifts my shirt over my head and tosses it, then spreads my legs with his knee. "I can't think about this." He kisses my left nipple. "Or this." He kisses my right one then takes it into his mouth. "If I think about this." He pushes inside of me and I melt into him. "I wouldn't last a day without you." Laine takes his time, enjoying every inch of my body.

***

I wake at three-thirty in the morning and find Laine standing at the window.

"Are you—" I stop. "What are you doing?"

His face is illuminated by the moon. "Just thinking."

"About what?"

"Where I'll be a month from now." I join him at the window. We look towards the beach and listen to the waves in the distance. He places his hand on my abdomen. "I want to know as soon as you find out."

"Of course."

"Email me and make sure you tell my parents; in case I call them first."

"They'll be the first to know."

"I hope it's a girl."

"Really?" I'm surprised by this. "You don't want a son?"

"Eventually, yes. But I really want a little Alee that's all mine. Only mine."

Benny was gone the first two years of our relationship. We never had to deal with him, or the past. Laine would never admit it, but he's jealous of my friendship with Benny. His jealousy makes him feel weak. He can't afford that, not now.

I rub my hand over my belly and plead with the universe. I need this. Laine needs this. We go back to bed and give it another go, just in case the first six times weren't enough.

***

After breakfast we go to the beach. Laine's parents walk hand in hand behind us, Cruz and Benny walk ahead of us. I'm glad they're getting along, for Laine's sake. When it's time to head back to base, Laine asks me to stay behind. He tells his parents that he wants Benny to drive them back. His father looks crestfallen, his mother cries. I tell him I understand. We say our goodbyes on the lawn. He kisses me long and deep, and makes me promise to eat real food for dinner. I say yes to everything. I'll do anything he asks as long as he promises to come home.

As Laine walks to Benny's rental car, his father stops him. He takes Laine by the shoulders and holds him there. "Don't be a hero, son." His words scare me. His mother, too. We look at each other with the same frightened

195

expression. We're all thinking it; I'm glad his father had the nerve to say it out loud.

Laine regards his father then hugs him. "Dad, I don't know how not to be." He smiles then ducks down to get into the car.

Laine is a hero; he doesn't need a uniform or a gun to prove it.

I TURN OFF
Chapter Twenty Five

I hand the salesclerk at the pharmacy counter forty dollars and wait for my change. She gives me back pennies and wishes me luck. I blush. Aren't these people trained not to comment on what guests are purchasing?

"Thanks," I mumble and walk out with the pregnancy tests. I hope two is enough. I read online you should take more than one to make sure you don't get a false positive. Two is more than one.

When I get home there's a note taped to the door in my mother's writing. It says she's gone to a center for treatment. It says she'll be gone thirty days. I sit on the porch with the note clutched in my hand. It isn't like I wanted to share my news with her. I don't even know if she'll care. The first time I got pregnant, she didn't speak to me for a month.

After the initial shock wears off, I start to feel almost hopeful. I'll need help. Laine's parents will be there for me, but it would be nice to have someone on my side who cares. Mom's never gone away for treatment. Maybe this time will be different.

I go inside and drop my keys on the side table and head to the bathroom. I place the tests in the cabinet. I don't need to hide them now. I shouldn't feel the need to hide them at all, but I still feel like a kid playing grown-up. For the most accurate result, it says I should wait to test my pee in the morning. An early night it is.

I'm changing into my pajamas when I hear my phone buzz in my backpack. I must have accidentally turned off the ringer again. I have four missed calls. Two from Laine's father, one from Mom, and one from Benny. Benny hasn't spoken to me since San Diego. After he took Laine and Cruz to the base, he came back to the house really tense. He said he was fine, that he had to fly back to New York immediately. I didn't question him. I figured he was upset— we all were. He texted me a few days later and said he was busy with school and not to take it personally if he was MIA for a while. I sent back a middle finger emoji. That was a month ago.

I put on Laine's USMC t-shirt and a pair of running shorts then sit on my bed contemplating who to call first and why each of these people has tried to reach me in the span of ninety minutes. Mom could've been calling to tell me she was leaving. That makes sense. Benny wouldn't call unless something was wrong. If he wanted to say hi, he would text. The two missed calls from Laine's father are the ones that scare me. My phone buzzes and my dilemma is averted. It's Benny. I stare at his goofy picture on my screen. He held the camera real close to his face, so it's all eyes, nose, and mouth. He wanted it to look like he was coming through the phone whenever he called. My finger hovers over the accept button. *Why doesn't he text me?*

I let the call go to voicemail. My phone vibrates with a message alert at the same time the doorbell rings. My heart kicks into action. *Maybe Laine is here. Maybe he's home.*

I run to the door, not really expecting to see him, but hoping like hell it's him. I open the door and find Bryn's mother, Frances, standing on the porch. Her face is pale; she's half the woman I knew her as. She was always plump; that's what my mom called her. She's wasted away in the years since Bryn's death.

"Oh my God, how are you." I give her a hug. "You look good," I add because that's what people say.

"I'm well." She ends the hugs, then looks at me poignantly. "How are you?"

"I'm good," I tell her. "Come in."

She places her purse on the side table. "It hasn't changed," she comments on the décor.

I laugh. "I know. It's still horrible."

She smiles and sits on the sofa. "Your mom called," she starts. "She asked me to check in on you while she's gone."

That was thoughtful of her but she just left. Frances didn't have to rush over this quickly.

"How are Laine's parents?"

I look at her in utter confusion. "Why would his parents care about Mom going to treatment?"

Before she has a chance to reply, the kitchen phone rings. Frances lowers her head and I realize that she's been crying. I answer the phone on the third ring. It's Laine's father. I wonder how he got our number, then I remember Mom kept our information public in case my father ever tried to find her. Us. Whatever.

"Alee, sweetie. Come over, please. We want you here with us." His voice is thick with pain.

Frances watches me from the sofa. "James, what's going on?"

"Oh God, you didn't hear... Benny didn't call..." He breaks down. He cries into the receiver, and I find it odd that I'm holding it together. I need to hear him say it. If he doesn't say the words, it isn't real. I can remain in this false reality another twenty seconds.

"There was an accident..."

I drop the phone. It bounces off my foot and lands with a thud. Frances asks if there is anything she can do.

"Is there someone you want me to contact who can stay with you?"

"I have nobody."

***

My phone jingles at two in the morning. I jump up thinking it's Laine. It will never be Laine again. It's Benny. He says he's at the front door. I get out of bed and head to the door. I'm surprised to find Frances asleep on the sofa. I thought she left hours ago. She wakes when I let Benny in.

"You don't have to stay," I tell her.

"Okay, but call if you need anything. You don't have to go through this alone."

I hope she doesn't think she owes me. I sat with her all those nights after Bryn died because I wanted to. Because I missed Bryn. I did it for me. I don't want her here out of pity. I want someone to swim in the pain with me. Someone who understands. I look at Benny, whose eyes are as red and swollen as mine. "I'm not alone."

Benny and I set up camp on the couch. He stays on one end and I curl up on the other side.

"I was walking out of a biology lab when I got the call. As soon as I saw the caller ID, I knew." He shakes his head.

"I fucking knew it." I reach for his hand. He leans closer to me. "You know what my first thought was?"

I shrug.

"I wanted to punch that dude Cruz in the face. I want to fucking nail him right in the nose." He squeezes my hand. "He promised to have his back." Benny clears his throat. "I guess it didn't matter though. No training can prepare you for a freak helicopter accident. James said he ran back to pull a civilian out of the way. He had to be a fucking hero."

I cry again. Benny cries too. We cry on the couch until dawn. Past dawn, until noon. I don't speak. I can't speak. I can barely breathe.

The doorbell rings and I jump from sleep. The room is dark, but it feels like evening. I can't move my legs; Benny is lying on top of them. "Benny, wake up." I wiggle my leg free. "Someone is at the door."

He stirs when the doorbell rings again. He springs from the couch, still half asleep as he opens the door. Laine's father is standing on my porch. James looks at Benny, then inside the house at me laid out on the couch. "Why didn't you come over? You can stay with us." James waits for me to speak; he doesn't know I lost my voice. I lost everything. "My wife really wants to see you. I'll wait here while you get some things together. Come on, get up." He takes my hand and helps me off the couch.

I go to my room and pack. I choose things I wore the last time Laine was home. Things that remind me of him. When I return to the living room, I find Benny and James holding each other. Benny is mumbling that he's sorry. James keeps saying it isn't his fault. It's nobody's fault. That isn't true. We're all to blame. We didn't allow Laine to grow; we held him back. If he had gone to UC Davis, if the city job had come through, if I was more ambitious, if I encouraged him more. He could have become a sheriff or a firefighter. He wouldn't have enlisted. He'd be here. Not lying in a body bag on the other side of the world.

***

Laine's body arrived at San Francisco International Airport two days ago. I didn't go to the airport or help with the funeral arrangements. I didn't take any calls or reply to a single text. I don't know how to exist in a world that doesn't include Laine.

I lie on his bed listening to his iPod. He has four playlists: Workout, Running, Sleep, Alee. I don't listen to the Alee list. I play the others on a loop. Someone knocks on the door, then opens it slowly. Benny appears in front of me.

"Hey, little bird." He runs his hand over my head. "You have to get up now." Benny is dressed in a black suit. It looks new, but he's probably had it awhile. Benny goes to events that require suits. Laine hated suits. He's probably wearing something the Marines issued now. They owned him. They killed him.

"Come on." Benny removes the blanket from my shoulder. "Do you need anything from your place?"

I shake my head and sit up. Benny leaves so I can get dressed. I realize I haven't showered in I don't know how long. I take a shower in Laine's bathroom. I cry when I pour shampoo in my hand. It smells like Laine. I wonder if I'll stop seeing him in every little thing. I hope not. I rinse my hair and run a bar of soap over my skin. I stop at my belly. Does it seem bigger, harder? I push it out. Nothing happens. I spent so many years avoiding pregnancy; now I want it more than anything in the world.

I wear the same dress I wore to Bryn's funeral. It's tight and feels shorter even though I haven't grown an inch since then. I'm too old for this style; I look stupid, but I don't care. This was the dress I wore the day I started to fall in love with Laine. I skip the black tights and slip on my boots with no socks. "You look like a whore," I say to the reflection.

"You look beautiful," it replies.

No. That wasn't the mirror. *Laine?*

"Let's go," Benny says from the door.

There is no church service, just a small gathering at Duggan's mortuary on Valencia. After that, we drive to the cemetery in San Bruno. Laine is buried in a long row of fallen soldiers. His headstone is plain white like the thousands of soldiers buried before him. It's inscribed with his name, rank, birthday and date of death. That's it.

Forty or so people follow us back the DiCaros. More arrive later in the day. By the time night falls, his father is very drunk. Not in a rowdy, loud way. He's quiet and brooding.

"Hide this." Janey shoves a half-empty bottle of bourbon into my hand. I take the bottle to Laine's room and leave it on the desk. Benny and one of Laine's cousins help James to bed. Slowly, people begin to leave. I spot Heather putting on her coat. She came over after her shift with a card signed by everyone at work. I thank her for coming, and she slips me a couple of pills.

"I take them for anxiety sometimes. One of these and a glass of wine will give you a good night's sleep." She hugs me. "You could really use the beauty sleep."

I actually smile at her comment. I like that she acknowledges my horrid appearance.

"Goodnight, Heather." I close the door and turn around to an empty room.

Janey has gone to bed. Her doctor gave her Valium, and she's been popping them every night to help her sleep. She offered me one, but I didn't want to deny her a night of rest. I look at the pills in my hand and debate on whether or not

I should take them. I really just want this day to be over. I want to sleep. More importantly, I want to forget. I take the pills with a sip of someone's leftover wine, then gather glasses from the living room and take them to the kitchen. The counters are peppered with half-empty casseroles dishes. As I load the dishwasher, I start to feel lightheaded. The pills are fast. I leave the kitchen and start down the hall. It's wavy, like a funhouse illusion. When I walk into the bedroom, Laine comes out of the bathroom.

Not Laine.

Benny.

I squint my eyes to shake the misperception from my thoughts. He lays his suit jacket over the desk chair and picks up the bourbon. He takes a pull straight from the bottle then offers it to me. I take the bottle and toss it back. I gag hard but keep it down. When the burning subsides, I do it again. The third and fourth go down smoothly. The room is swaying like the deck of a ship. I carefully place the bottle on the desk and try to gain my bearings.

Benny takes his tie off and throws it beside the bottle. His sleeves are rolled up, and his shirt is untucked. His face morphs into Laine the day of Bryn's funeral, then back to Benny.

"You have to leave." My tongue is heavy, my speech comes out in thick, choppy words. "I want to change."

"Change in the bathroom." He motions towards the illuminated doorway behind him.

I grab my clothes from the end of the bed and walk towards the light. I lean on the sink and look at my reflection. The room pulsates. I need to lie down. I toss my dress on the floor and slip on the clothes in my hand.

Laine is on the bed. No. Benny is on the bed. Music oozes from the stereo. I don't need to check the iPod to know this is the *Alee* list. A fist reaches into my chest and squeezes until I can't breathe. My sobs come in waves. Painful, agonizing waves. My throat burns, my chest aches, my legs give out. I close my eyes and let the deep melody and the soothing tone of Al Green's voice guide me into a dream.

His arms wrap around me. *He's holding me.* I turn over and bury my face in his neck. I tell him I love him. I miss him. I'm sorry. I ask him if this is real. He whispers yes. It was just a dream. A horrible dream. He's on top of me. His tongue invades my mouth. His hands rip at my sweats. I arch to make it easier for him to pull them off. He tells me he loves me. *He loves me so fucking much.* I feel him peel each layer of clothing off his body. His shirt, his pants, his boxers. When I feel his warmth between my legs, I open my eyes.

The world is not what it seems.

Reality is crushing my ribs. He's breathing heavily into my hair.

"Benny," I say. "Benny, stop."

He whispers my name and pushes his knee into my inner thigh to spread my legs.

"Please, Benny," I cry and push on his chest. Maybe he's lost in a dream, too. Maybe he doesn't know what he's doing. "It's me. It's Alee," I plead.

"I love you, Alee," he cries. He's crying, sobbing. "I've always loved you. And you love me."

I push against him, punching at his chest, his neck, his face. He grabs my hands and holds them between us. I've never felt more weak, more hopeless.

"You want me. I know you want me."

"I love Laine. I want Laine," I say through gritted teeth.

His head falls into the pillow. He cries, but he doesn't let me go.

"Benny, get off of me," I speak softly. Lovingly. If I don't fight him, maybe he'll stop. He'll come to his senses and stop.

"I'm sorry, Alee." He lets my hands go and holds himself above me. "Oh shit, I'm so fucking sorry."

"It's okay," I tell him. I'll say anything to make this stop.

I wait for Benny to roll off me. He doesn't. He holds himself between my legs. My body shivers. The movement seems to snap something in his head. I can't see his face; the room is too dark. I make out the faint outline of his mouth, his eyes. He's staring at me, through me.

"Benny," I whisper. Before I can think of what to say next, he falls on top of me, crushing me. My first thought is that he passed out. That's how heavy he is. Then I feel movement. His hips rise, then he pushes forward.

"Benny, no!" I yell. Not loud enough to wake anyone. Not loud enough to call for help. I want him to stop on his own. I don't want Janey or James to walk in here and see what he's doing to me. I don't want them to blame me.

He pulls out and pushes against me again.

"Stop," I say through my tears with what little air he is allowing me to inhale. "Benny." I exhale his name as he slams into me again. His name comes out as a whimper. Something that sounds sensual.

"Alee," he moans back. "Goddamn, baby. I missed you so much."

I don't say another word. I don't move. I barely breathe. I start to fall asleep. The pills, the booze. I turn off.

NOT IN THE MOOD FOR BRUNCH

Chapter Twenty Six

I wake in a haze to the smell of his cologne. I don't move, I just listen. For breathing. Movement. I hear nothing. Absolutely nothing. My eyes flicker open. Light forces its way into the room from behind the window blinds. Laine's parents will be up soon. I don't want them to see me. Him. Us. I turn slowly; every inch feels like an eternity. When I'm flat on my back, I force myself to look.

Benny is gone.

I throw the comforter off and run to the bathroom. I turn on the shower and step in before the water is hot. I scrub my skin with Laine's bar soap until the water is so hot it scalds me. I let it. I shower until the water turns cold again. I don't even wash my hair. I just rinse. Rinse it all away.

"Alee," Janey calls from the other side of the door. She knocks softly and walks in. "Are you okay?" She's never walked in on me showering before. I hope Benny isn't the kitchen blabbing about how we slept together. He isn't that stupid. "The water has been on for over an hour. I just wanted to make sure you were okay."

Laine asked me to stop asking him if he was okay. I get it now. I see. I see so much more. "Everything is fine." I turn off the water.

She tells me they're going to the grocery store. "For as much food as people dropped off, we don't have anything for breakfast, and we're out of creamer." She asks if I want anything particular for lunch.

I hope she doesn't think I'm staying. I can't stay here. Not now. Not ever again. "Um, is anyone else here?" I can't even say his name. I don't want to be in this house alone with him.

"Everyone is gone. It's just us. We'll lock up when we leave. Take your time." She closes the door and I fall to the shower floor.

I somehow find the strength to get up and dry myself off. Laine's room is no longer the sanctuary it once was. I don't look at the bed. I don't even touch it as I search my bag for clean, untarnished clothes. I put on the Thanksgiving outfit.

Why did I let Benny do that to me? This is my fault. I wasn't clear about how I felt. What I wanted. *Did I flirt with him? Lead him on?* Did I give Benny the wrong impression or worse, did I give him permission? I grab my head and scream.

I rip the comforter and sheets off the bed and drag them to the laundry room. I shove them in the washer, toss in two pods, and set the cycle on hot. I march back to Laine's room. *Laine's room.* I fucked Benny in Laine's room. In his bed. I fall to my knees and cry into the mattress.

You stupid bitch! You stupid fucking bitch!

My teeth grind together so hard it feels as if my jaw will crack. I pull my wet hair with both hands and pull until the nerves in my head throb. The rage, the guilt, the disgust is too much. I bang my head on the hardwood. I bang until my ears throb. I'm still on the floor when Laine's parents return. My head feels like it weighs a hundred pounds. I compose myself as best as I can and pack my bag. When I find my sweats and the USMC t-shirt on the floor beside the bed, I stop. Benny's hands ripping at my clothes. The t-shirt coming over my head, the sweats sliding down my legs. *I let him. I let him undress me.* I walk out of the room, leaving the shirt and sweats behind.

"Coffee should be done in a few minutes," James says when I walk past the kitchen. "You want a bagel? We got

212

Noah's." He holds up the brown paper bag. "I got that schmear you like." He references the garden vegetable spread I craved the first time I was pregnant.

"I have to go." My voice barely above a whisper, hoarse from screaming.

"Alee, wait." Janey chases after me. "Where are you going?"

"Home." It's the last place I ever want to be. It's cold and deserted. It's a house of painful memories and lies. It's where I belong.

"But, why?" She looks as if she may cry. "You can stay here. With us."

I can't stay here, not ever. Not after what happened last night. "I want to start getting back to normal." As if there is a normal. I don't know how to live life with Laine. I didn't exist before him. Not this version of me. The one who knew love and loved with her whole heart. That Alee died the moment Laine drew his last breathe.

She pulls me into her arms. This is the last time she'll ever hold me. We have no reason to hug or care about each other now. The rope tethering our lives has been cut. We're on our own.

"Our door is always open. Always." She returns to the kitchen.

James walks to the door. "Come by for dinner on Sunday." He starts back to the kitchen then turns around. "Benny and his mom will be here, too. You can say goodbye before he goes back to school."

Fuck, Benny. I fucked Benny.

I don't go home. I run to the wall hoping Hawk is there. Hoping his offer to kick Benny's ass still stands. The wall is empty and wet from the morning fog. I wander the streets, searching for him in dark corners. Hawk, my father, is nowhere to be found. Even the birds have abandoned me.

I see a somewhat familiar face waiting for the bus. I've seen him around the neighborhood over the years, although we've only spoken once. I stop beside him and look up the street for a bus I don't plan on catching.

"Hi," he says.

"Hi."

"I haven't seen you in a while."

"Were you looking?"

"Actually, I was. How's your friend? The one who fucked your ex."

"She's dead."

He laughs at first then realizes I'm not smiling. "Oh my God, you're serious?"

I nod.

"I'm so sorry." He steps closer and stands in front of me as if he's going to hug me.

"It happened a while ago." I don't mention the details. He doesn't need to know she was the girl killed in the Balboa Pool shooting.

"You look upset." It's a nice way to say you look like you've been in bed crying for six days.

"My fiancé died." I don't know why I'm telling him this. Why I'm being so blasé about it all. Just stating it as simple fact. It's almost liberating, therapeutic. I feel detached from the hurt and pain.

"How?" He takes another step closer.

"Afghanistan."

He shakes his head and says, "Man, I'm so sorry."

I look around him. "The bus is coming."

It stops at the sidewalk, and people line up to board. He steps into place at the back of the line. "You're not getting on?"

"I'm not waiting for the bus."

"Then why are you standing at the bus stop?"

"I don't want to be alone." There are people not far from here who care about me, who would welcome me with open arms. I choose to be with strangers. The cold, uncaring company of people who don't know my name. I'm my father's daughter.

215

He steps out of line and the bus pulls away. We stand in silence for three rounds of red lights. On the fourth light, someone joins us at the bus stop. He pulls out his cell phone and types a text, then puts it back in his pocket.

"I'm Court." He holds out his hand.

"I'm Alee." We shake hands. His are cold, mine are colder.

"Nice to meet you, Alee. So, do you do this often?" He chuckles in a nervous kind of way. "I have to admit, this is a first for me?"

"What? Talking about dead fiancés isn't typical bus stop chit-chat?"

"Hiding at bus stops to avoid dealing with painful situations."

"Are you avoiding a painful situation?"

"I guess you can say that."

"Are you a shrink?"

"No, I'm an English teacher." He points down the street. "I teach eighth grade English at James Lick Middle School. But I did minor in psychology."

"Just my luck." Another woman joins our growing group. The bright pink floral Billabong tote hanging from her shoulder reminds me of Bryn. "Do you believe in fate, Court?"

"I do. Not to the point where I let it run my life. I think if something is meant to be it will be. Ultimately, we control the outcome of our lives."

"A simple yes or no would've been sufficient."

Court laughs.

"My boyfriend's name was Laine. My name is Alee. Your name is Court. All we're missing is Street and Boulevard."

"That's kind of awesome."

In no way do I believe Court was brought to me as some kind of sign. His name was given to him long before I was born. He doesn't look much older than me, but I assume he is, given his profession and the way he carries himself.

"How old are you?"

Court pauses a moment and looks down at me. I can tell he's trying to figure me out. I read once that men classify women into two categories: fuckable and non-fuckable. Maybe the article didn't use those terms, but that was the point. Within fifteen minutes of meeting someone, a guy knows if he wants to have sex. Court isn't sure about me. Not yet.

"I'm thirty-nine. How old are you?"

"Twenty-one."

I see him nod in my peripheral vision. A large neon fuckable sign just appeared above my head.

"Are you married?" I ask him.

"Divorced. Actually, the day I saw you here I was headed to meet my lawyer."

"Interesting."

"Why is that interesting?" He's intrigued by our banter.

"That particular day I was newly single and I ran into you at this bus stop. Now, I'm newly single again and here we are."

"Interesting." He takes a sidestep closer to me. "Is it fate?"

"It's definitely something."

Court and I hang out at the bus stop for an hour. When the ninth bus passes by, his phone rings.

"It's my sister. Today is her birthday. I'm supposed to be at her house for brunch."

"That's the painful situation you're trying to avoid?"

"You haven't met my sister," Court smirks. "I don't suppose you want to come with me?"

"No."

"It's not a formal thing. We're just getting together in her backyard."

"I'm not in the right state of mind for brunch."

"Nobody is ever in the right state of mind for brunch. That's what the booze is for."

"I look terrible."

He checks me out. "The outfit is on fleek."

"Did you just say *fleek?*"

"I spend my days with thirteen-year-olds. You pick up the lingo."

I like his honesty. I decide to give him a dose of honesty in return. "I buried my fiancé yesterday then had questionably consensual sex with his best friend last night. At his parents' house, in his bed. So I'm not sure if brunch is where I should be right now."

Court regards me for a moment, not sure if I'm serious or just being ironic. "Are you okay?"

"If we're going to be friends, you have to promise me one thing."

"Anything."

"Don't ever ask me if I'm okay."

"Okay."

We take the bus to Court's sister's house. Actually, we take the bus, then a train. When we get off the train, I ask Court why he doesn't drive.

"Parking sucks on my street."

"You're too old to take the bus."

"I am not."

"You are. Maybe that's why your wife left."

"She didn't leave because I don't drive. She left because I slept with her sister."

I stop walking and look at Court with total judgment. "You're a fucking douche."

"Says the girls who had sex with her dead fiancé's best friend." Court stops in front of a gray stucco house in the middle of the block. "We're here."

His sister has a nice house and the kind of backyard you see photographed in *Sunset Magazine*. Concrete and stone with accents of foliage around the edge of the yard. There are at least thirty people milling around sipping mimosas when we arrive. They all stop to gawk at Court and the manic-looking girl he brought with him. Court waves arrogantly and goes straight for the alcohol. When people ask how we met, Court doesn't lie. I like that.

"We met at the bus stop a few years ago. Then we reconnected today at the same bus stop," he tells his sister, Meagan. The birthday girl.

Someone calls Court away, leaving Meagan and me alone near her lemon tree.

"So you've known Court a few years?" she probes.

"Nearly four, I think." I pick up a fallen lemon. I hold it to my nose to mask the smell of bullshit.

"If you don't mind my asking, how old are you?"

I toss the lemon back into the brush. It will shrivel up and die soon. Everything dies. "Twenty-one."

She chokes on her mimosa. "So you were only seventeen when you met Court."

"My senior year in high school." I sip my virgin mimosa.

"Excuse me," she says and marches straight to Court and pulls him into the house.

I think I got Court in trouble. Time to go.

I pick a croissant off a silver tray on the buffet. I move a little farther down and take a blueberry muffin. I wrap my snacks in a napkin then drink the rest of my juice. I place the glass on the table and head for the exit. Court walks out just as I'm about to escape through the side gate.

"Let's get out of here." He opens the gate and we leave. "Where do you want to go?"

"Home."

Court comes back to the house with me. I tell him Mom is in rehab as I unlock the door.

"I did a little time in rehab. Coke and pills," he says as he steps inside. "What's your mom's poison?"

"Bourbon and the past." I drop my keys on the side table. "So, why was your sister freaking out?"

He sits on the sofa and pats the spot beside him. I sit down. "She thinks our relationship is inappropriate."

"We aren't having a relationship so why would she think that?" I unzip my boots and pull them off.

"Because I have a history of inappropriate relationships."

"Well, I'm not your sister-in-law."

"But you're young." He pauses. "She was only eighteen when we slept together. Actually, I slept with her when she was sixteen. They don't know that. In fact, I've never admitted that to anyone."

I'm not impressed by his confession. "How does someone your age end up sleeping with your sixteen-year-old sister-in-law?"

"We were camping with my wife's family. She was in my tent looking for sunblock and found my coke stash. She threatened to out me unless I gave her a taste. We told my wife and in-laws we were going swimming, and I took her half a mile down the river. I let her snort a line off my hand. Then I fucked her in the woods."

"You're a bigger prick than I originally thought." I totally mean it as an insult, and he doesn't seem to mind. I like that. He knows what he is. He doesn't deny it.

"It gets worse," he says with absolutely no remorse. "We flirted on and off for the next few years. On her eighteenth birthday, she got drunk and came to our house. She knew my wife was at her best friend's bachelorette party. The second I let her in, she was all over me. Touching, grabbing. I fucked her up against the wall in the living room. Her face was right next to our wedding picture." He recalls with a shit-eating grin. Just when I think he can't actually get

222

worse, there's more. "A month later my wife tells me her sister is pregnant. That she knows it's mine and my marriage was over."

"Do you have a kid somewhere in the world?" I can't imagine a more fucked up parent. Wait. Yes. I can.

He smiles. "Her name is Rue."

"Rue?"

"Yeah, my sister-in-law is a big *Hunger Games* fan."

At least he's in his daughter's life. It's a redeeming quality. "That still doesn't explain why your sister freaked out about me."

"My former in-laws tried to get me fired from my job. Saying I was a sexual predator. They just wanted to hurt me like I hurt them. But nothing stuck. She never told them about the woods or the coke. The sex we had on her birthday was *consensual*." He gives me a look.

I ignore it. I like listening to Court's drama. Court's drama is more interesting than mine. Because it isn't mine. I don't want to talk about myself, not today.

Court buys tacos for dinner. We eat them on the sofa. At eight o'clock, the living room is dark. I don't get up to turn on the light. We sit in darkness and stare out the window.

"I should go," he says.

"If you think you should."

"Do you want me to go?"

"I don't want to make any decisions. If you think you should go, then go. If you want to stay, then stay. You can sleep in my mother's room."

Court laughs. "Really?"

"Yes." I realize I don't even know when she's due back. It doesn't really matter. Even when she's home, she's not here. "I just decided something."

"What's that." Court has half a smile on his face. A hopeful one, like my decision has something to do with where he sleeps. Technically, Court hasn't made a move on me. No inappropriate touching or flirting for that matter. He's just here, existing with me.

"I'm going to treat each day as a new life. I wake up, live that day, then die every night just to be reborn again in the morning. It's the only way I can be in this world. At least until I find something to live for."

Court frowns and places his arm on the back of the couch. "That's a lot of living and dying for someone your age."

"Maybe I won't feel this way forever. There is no forever. Just for now."

"I want to stay," Court says.

"Then stay."

HE DOESN'T HAVE AGE APPROPRIATE FRIENDS

Chapter Twenty Seven

I haven't left the house since the day I brought Court home. He goes to school in the mornings, then returns at night with dinner. Chinese, Mexican, McDonald's. He never comes back empty-handed. Court is very thoughtful. We eat while he grades papers at the dining room table and we talk about his students. His day. His life.

On the sixth day, someone knocks on the door at four fifteen. It's not Court. It's Bryn's mom. She has a bag of groceries. I let her in and tell her I'm expecting company.

"I just wanted to drop these by and give you an update on your mom." She places a carton of strawberry ice cream in the freezer and sets a ten-pack of ramen noodles on the counter. "She extended her stay another two weeks, possibly four."

"It must be nice to run away." I walk to the sink and place my empty coffee mug inside.

"She's not running anymore, Alee." Frances walks to the sink. "She's healing."

I shrug and turn the water on to rinse my mug. "Thanks for the food, but it isn't necessary. I'm doing fine. A friend is staying with me."

Frances narrows her eyes. "Is it Benny?"

His name ignites the memory. *His weight pressing me into the bed. Pressing into me. His breath on my neck...*

"No," I snap.

Frances picks up one of Court's shirts and places it on the messy dining room table. Evidence of a male presence is strewn throughout the living room. A pair of hiking boots, Sports Illustrated magazine, empty beer bottles. "Sorry. It's none of my business. I'll get out of your hair."

I feel bad for the outburst, but I let her leave without apologizing. Court shows up twenty minutes later with sandwiches from Roxie's. I tell him my mom extended her treatment and asks what his plans are for the holidays.

"I have my daughter this weekend, but I'll be back on Monday. Will you be okay?" Court piles yesterday's Chinese food cartons in a bag and carries them to the kitchen.

"I'll survive." I rest my head on the table feeling a little queasy. "I ate too much." Court puts his hand to my forehead. "You don't look good." He pulls my chair out. "Why don't you go to bed. I'll clean up."

Court is the closest thing to a best friend I've had in a long time. I'm drawn to the darkness in him. He's so fucked up it makes me feel like a better person. It's more than that. He keeps me from being alone.

Court doesn't return on Monday. It's winter break so he doesn't have class. I don't text him. We don't have that kind of relationship. We don't have a relationship.

On Wednesday I wake to someone knocking on the door. I went to bed with a stomachache and I still don't feel well. The knocking continues. I roll out of bed and feel the contents of my dinner—hot Cheetos and a Diet Coke—creep towards the back of my throat. I barely make it to the toilet. I heave orange chunks into the water then sit back against the cabinet. The bathroom is filthy. Court has bad aim. I flush the toilet and open the cabinet to get cleanser. The plastic bag, the one with the white and pink box falls to the floor. I've given up all hope and desire to use the test. At this point, it would be a cruel joke.

Fuck it.

I open the package and sit on the toilet with the stick between my legs. I leave it on the sink, then answer the door. It's Court's sister.

"Is my brother here?"

"No."

"Have you seen him today?"

"No."

"Hasn't he been staying here, with you?"

"Sort of. I haven't seen him since last Friday."

"Please have him call me if he comes by."

"Okay."

I call Court. He answers on the first ring.

"Hey, Alee, what's up?"

"Your sister came over."

"What? Why? What did you tell her?"

"That you aren't here."

"That's it?"

"That's all there is to tell," I say. I hear him shush someone in the background. "Where are you?"

"With a friend."

"A friend?"

"Yes."

"An age-appropriate friend?"

"Alee, come on. You of all people should understand life is complicated." He sighs into the receiver. "We love each other."

I hang up on Court before he says something I can't unhear.

***

It's three hours before I remember the test on the sink. I close my eyes and pick it up. I don't know what I'm hoping to find. An image of Benny flashes in my mind. My teeth grind into each other. *Me. Benny.* That was two weeks ago. It's too soon to be pregnant by Benny.

I open my eyes and find one line. One faint pink line of disappointment.

F★CK THE
HOLIDAYS
Chapter Twenty Eight

It turns out Court is a liar. And a pedophile. Sort of. He doesn't get off on naked pics of kids. He just likes fucking underage girls. I find this out a week after I learned I'm not pregnant with Laine's baby. The pregnancy test was negative but I still haven't gotten my period. I read online it could be due to stress. I've been under a lot of stress.

Court's sister, Meagan, came by again yesterday, which was also Christmas Eve. She told me Court was running an ad on Craigslist offering tutoring services. He met the girls with the intention of tutoring them. If they seemed open to more, he gave them more. Court is a creepy Craigslist dude. Meagan says Court and one of these students have been gone for almost four days. Her parents have contacted the police. Court told me he had his daughter for the weekend, apparently, he had someone else's daughter.

My phone rings from the nightstand and I reach over to get it. It's a text from Court. He's at the front door.

"Alee." He steps inside and hugs me. He never hugs me. "It isn't as bad as they're making it seem."

"So, you didn't run away with an underage girl?"

"No!" he yells. I step back. "I never forced anyone to do something they didn't want to do."

I think about that statement. "Define force."

"Coercing a person to do something against their will."

"Or against their better judgment."

"No, that's not the same."

"So putting someone in a situation where they react in a way that is against their better judgment because they don't feel like they can say no, isn't that force?"

"By definition, no."

"By basic human emotion. Fight or flight. Survive or die. Yes, or no. When you coerce someone into a situation where they feel the need to justify how they got there. That is another kind of force. It doesn't have to be physical."

"I'm sorry you feel that way, Alee." He walks to the door. "I really hope things work out for you." He pauses with his hand on the doorknob. "Do me a favor?"

"Sure."

"If the police come to question you, be honest about me. About who I am."

"I will."

He walks out and I lock the door.

I go back to bed and fall into a deep sleep. In my dream, Laine is alive. He kisses my cheeks as we lay in a field of damp grass. A violin wales in the background, playing a song I recognize but can't remember the name. My dreams are vivid, yet fake. I'm not really sleeping; I'm remembering. Memories are dangerous. They can trap a person in the past, hold a life hostage. Just ask my mother.

I force myself out of bed at three. It's Christmas Day. I promised Laine's parents I would have dinner with them. I shower and dress in a pair of jeans and a fluffy, light gray V-neck sweater. Laine used to call it Snowball.

I stop at Walgreens. It's the only place open. I'm the only shopper inside. I pick up a Magic Bullet mini blender for Janey. This one comes with a handy to-go mug. I'm torn between the Stufz Burger maker and the Chia Pet in the shape of Abraham Lincoln's head for James. I buy both along with gift bags and tissue that are on clearance for fifty percent off. I assemble the gift bags in the parking lot then walk the familiar route to Laine's house. Christmas decorations adorn the neighborhood. Even the DiCaro's strung lights on their porch.

"Alee," Janey half greets, half announces to the rest of the house that I've arrived. I didn't anticipate seeing other people. It's an idiotic notion. Of course the entire Dicaro family is here. What's left of them anyway. "I feel like I haven't seen you in forever." Janey gives me another squeeze.

Days blend into each other. Time is a blurred concept. One month ago I was with Laine. Two weeks ago I met Court. I've lived fourteen lives since then. Every day a new Alee is born, each one more fucked up than the last.

I settle in the kitchen and chat with Janey while she finishes preparing her mashed potatoes. She asks how I've been. I lie and tell her I went back to work. That I've been busy. I don't tell her about Court. She won't understand. I don't even get it. My feelings for Court are indifferent. Indifference is good. Indifference doesn't hurt. Having Court around keeps me from slipping further into darkness. Looking forward to his arrival gives me purpose, a reason to wake up, brush my teeth. I have no feelings about Court, he's just there. Was there.

Right before dinner is served, the doorbell rings again. I hear a loud greeting and assume it's more of Laine's cousins. It isn't until I see Beverly walk into the kitchen that I realize I'm wrong. My entire body freezes.

He's here. Benny is here.

"Alee," Beverly says. "I'm so happy to see you."

I don't know how, but I stand and hug her. My body is on autopilot.

"You look tired." Beverly's not subtle at all. Then again subtly was never her style.

"You look well-rested."

Beverly takes my snide remark as an actual compliment. "Thank you, sweetie."

Bev forces Janey to relinquish some of the dinner duties. Janey asks her to finish the salad and winks at me.

"So, Alee, how have you been?" Bev sits across from me with the salad ingredients. "Benny tells me nothing. That boy has been so focused on school, he barely calls."

The sound of his name causes a tickle at the back of my neck.

"Alee, can you take this to the dining room for me?" Janey hands me a platter filled with roasted vegetables.

He's somewhere in the house. I can feel it. I can smell him.

An extra table is set up in the dining room. It's filled with cheese and crackers, a few dips, and the spreadable cheese I ate at Benny's father's funeral. The thought of it makes me nauseous. I place the platter down and a hand touches my shoulder.

"Can we talk?" he whispers.

I don't want to cause a scene. I can't let these people find out what happened. I follow Benny down the hall into Laine's room. The comforter and pillows are lined up perfectly. There are two folded pieces of clothing sitting at the end of the bed. I pick up the shirt and smell it. It smells like nothing. Because it is nothing. Just a shirt. It isn't Laine.

"I'm so fucking sorry, Alee." Benny's voice cracks.

I exhale when I hear his apology.

"It never should have happened. It was completely my fault." Benny steps towards me.

"I forgive you. But don't ever touch me again." My pain, my rage, forces Benny back. For the first time in our lives, he hears me.

Benny tells everyone he isn't feeling well and leaves before dinner is served. I stay and eat. A lot. I eat until the top button of my jeans digs into my belly button. I open it and go back for dessert.

Janey asks me to stay over. I tell her I can't. "I hate to think of you in that empty house," she says.

"Mom will be home soon." I wrap my scarf around my neck. "These are for you." I hand her the gift bags. "It's just something I picked up for you and James."

"I'm sure they're wonderful," she says and hugs me. "Merry Christmas, Alee."

"Merry Christmas."

I don't make a big deal about leaving. When I pass the living room, Laine's dad sees me in my coat. He just smiles and nods. I do the same before I walk out the door. The night wasn't as horrible as I thought it would be. During dinner, Laine's cousins told a few stories from their childhood. Nobody dwelled on his absence. I don't know if that was for my benefit or his parents'. Hell, maybe people have just moved on.

***

I go back to work on New Year's Day. It's cold and raining. It's also really busy. My shift flies by. Heather offers me a ride home and I take it.

"How are you holding up?"

"I'm good," I tell her. "Just really tired."

"How are you sleeping?" She changes lanes and nearly sideswipes a Mini Cooper. "I can give you something to help."

"No." I've had enough of her pills.

The next day I'm sick as hell. The weather, the exhaust fumes. Something isn't right. I'm on my second emergency break to the bathroom. This is the third time I've puked today. The first was in the bushes outside the BART station on my way to work. As I'm walking out of the breakroom, my supervisor tells me to go home. I can't stomach public transportation, so I Uber. It costs a fortune. What do I need money for? I have no plans to move out or move on. Now mom and I can be alone together.

I open the front door and smell something burning. My mother walks into the living room with a spatula in her hand.

"You're home," I state the obvious.

She looks good. Healthy, lean, and happy. It pisses me off. I don't ask about her vacation. I'll never ask. While she was getting "healthy," my life was falling apart.

"Is everything okay?" She looks past me like someone else should be walking into the house. "Did something happen at work?"

"I'm sick." I drop my keys on the table. "What are you cooking?"

She looks at the spatula, then runs back to the kitchen. I follow her.

"Are you frying chicken?"

"Yes."

"Why?"

"It's my turn to bring a snack to group." She turns the heat off and plucks the nearly burnt, overly breaded lumps of chicken out of the oil and places them on a paper-towel-lined plate.

"Your turn?" I ask. "You just got back."

She moves the chicken to a plastic container.

"I've been staying with Frances." She clears her throat and opens the cabinet to find the lid to the container. I move her out of the way and open a drawer. I hand her the lid and slam the drawer shut.

I'm free-falling and she decided to stay away an extra two-weeks. My mother is sober for now, but being clean doesn't make you a decent human being. She's still fucked up. She's still fucking me up.

"I can leave you some chicken for dinner if you want."

Grease soaks the paper towel beneath the overly breaded chicken. "No, thanks. I'm not hungry..." I barely get the words out before I feel my chest heave. I run to the bathroom and drop to my knees in front of the toilet. My throat burns, my head throbs. I'm tired of feeling this way. Hopeless and sick. I flush the toilet and turn on the sink to brush my teeth. I wet my toothbrush and remember I used the last of the toothpaste this morning. I open the cabinet and find three boxes of toothpaste stacked on top of each other. Before Mom left, she started using Amazon Pantry. Buying in bulk is another one of her addictions. I grab a box and start to close the cabinet. I catch a glimpse of a pink and white box as the door shuts. I reach in and pull it out.

Fuck it.

I FOUND JESUS
Chapter Twenty Nine

Reginald finally tells me Hawk is in Portland. "He goes to this shit hole called The Basin. It's a dangerous place. Your old man told me he got fucked up there. That he would never go back."

"Then why do you think he's there now?"

"Punishment."

The word hits me in my core. He's punishing himself because of me. I must have stirred up a lot of shit. "If you ever see him again, tell him I'm sorry. That I don't blame him for anything." I stop walking and pull money out of my pocket. "Here, take this."

I hand him two hundred dollars in fives. I know it's easier for him to have smaller bills.

Reginald shakes his head adamantly. "No. No, I can't."

"I want you to have it. Save it for a really cold night and get a room." I shove the money towards his hand.

"I can't, Alee." He looks up apologetically. "If I take the money, I'll kill myself getting high."

I swallow the words I was just going to say. You can't argue with that. He finally agrees to take twenty-five. When he isn't looking, I sneak another fifty into the pocket of his jacket. He'll find it one day and thank me.

An hour later I'm sitting on a BART train thinking about Reginald. As destitute as he may seem, he still wants to live, and I can't for the life of me figure out why.

***

The following week I go to our meeting spot on Wednesday instead of Thursday. Reginald spends Wednesdays at a shelter so he can shower. I don't want to run into him today. He might try to stop me.

I see the guy with the sores lying on the cement wall behind the entrance to the station. Pigeons jump around him, shit on him; he doesn't move. He's the one they all buy drugs from. He's also the one Reginald said was the rapist.

The birds run to me when I approach the wall. I have nothing to feed them today. I'm on a mission. They flock around my feet when I stop in front of Jesus. They squawk warnings, I ignore them. What do they know, their just birds.

"Hey!" I'm not polite. You can't be. "Hey, Jesus!"

He flinches and almost falls off the wall.

"What the fuck?" He squints at me and shields his eyes with his filthy hand. Jesus has seen me around; I have some credibility. He also knows Hawk is my father. I'm hoping that buys me from safety.

"I need some shit."

He rolls off the wall and lands on his feet, motioning for me to follow him. Jesus looks like he could be eighteen, but he points out an elementary school as we walk to the park and says he went there twenty years ago, before the fucking hipsters ruined his hood. I tell him I grew up in Noe Valley. He nods some sort of approval then turns into the park.

"This used to be a shitty playground with a fucked-up baseball field. Now look at this." He waves his hand toward the four perfectly manicured soccer fields. "Dogs can't even shit in this park anymore. What the fuck is the world coming to?"

I want to ask him if he plays soccer, but it seems racist. I don't say anything. I just follow him, like a fucking idiot. He finally stops in the far corner of the park where a group of bushes lines up against a wooden fence. He crawls into the bushes; a few seconds later his brown hand appears, motioning for me to join him. It's only noon; nobody will be in this park until after three. I'll be raped by then. Multiple times.

"Are you fuckin' coming or what?" He peeks out and looks around. "I don't have all fucking day. Do you want the shit or not?"

He doesn't have all day. Really? "Do you have a meeting to get to?" I snap.

"Fuck this," he grumbles. He's about to crawl out when I stop him. If he's willing to back out, maybe he doesn't want to rape me.

"Wait." I take a deep breath. I'm too far gone to turn back now. "I'm coming in."

ARE YOU POSITIVE?

Chapter Thirty

I sit in a paper gown waiting for the nurse—doctor? I don't even know what she is—to come back with my test results. I lift my left leg and peel the paper off of my sweaty thigh. You'd think after years of technological advances, they would have something better than tissue paper to cover this table. The door opens and the nurse/doctor walks in. She's not smiling. Is that good or bad?

"So, you are most definitely pregnant." She sits on the round stool and spins away from the desk to look me in the eye. I like that. "Would you like to hear your options or do you plan to keep the baby?"

The news doesn't surprise me. The stick I peed on revealed two fat pink lines. My pants are snug, I vomit every hour, and I'm tired. So tired.

"What are my options?"

She spins back to the desk and flips through my chart. "The first day of your last period was November fifteenth, so that puts you at about nine and a half weeks. You're still in your first trimester, so we can give you a pill..."

"I'm sorry, what?" I interrupt her. "I'm how many weeks pregnant?"

She refers to her notes again. "About nine or ten."

"Are you sure? I took a test last month and it was negative."

"When was that?" She looks at the calendar on the wall.

"About a week before Christmas." I point to dates on the calendar without emotion. They're just numbers printed on a page. They mean nothing.

"How many tests did you take?"

"One."

"It might have been a false negative." She consults my questionnaire. "It says your last sexual partner was right around the time your period was due."

"Yes." I shiver. "I was under a lot of stress." I clear my throat.

"It could've been stress or just too soon for a test. Did you have unprotected sex from here to here." She points to the week of Thanksgiving and then two weeks later.

"Yes."

"And you missed your period in December."

"Yes."

I could've been pregnant the night of Laine's funeral.

"There are several factors that could've prevented you from having your period in December. There is some irregularity after a miscarriage, so your dates could have been off. But the most likely cause would be pregnancy."

I smile. Then start to cry. Big, fat, happy tears.

"Do you need a minute?" She places her hand on my shoulder.

"No." I sniffle.

She starts to rattle off my options again.

"No, I don't need options." I wipe my nose with the sleeve of my hoodie. "I'm keeping the baby."

If there is even an inkling of a chance this is Laine's child, I have something to live for. Something to look forward to. Someone to love.

I go straight to Laine's house and tell his parents I'm pregnant. They cry and hold me. It's the most love I've felt in a long time. They insist I stay with them. I tell them I can't. His mother seems very concerned about my aversion to stay. I tell her my mom needs me. She doesn't ask again. I go to work the next day and tell my boss. She makes note of my due date and we discuss the maternity leave process. Heather congratulates me and says she knows a great pregnancy yoga studio. As if.

After work, I walk up 24th Street and stop at the hipster baby store. I buy a pair of socks that look like Converse. I buy them in pink. Pink feels right. When I walk outside, I see Court across the street. He's walking behind a group of girls. Young girls. They turn around and giggle at something he says.

"Court!" I yell. It's more of a scolding.

He jumps—like, literally jumps. His eyes meet mine and he grins. He walks across the street, his teacher bag slung over his shoulder. He hugs me. I don't hug him back.

He acknowledges the bag from the baby store in my hand. "Are you?"

"I am."

"Congratulations?"

"Yes, thank you."

"Father?"

"It's complicated."

"I would expect nothing less from you."

"I see you've moved on to following girls home from school."

246

"They're my students. That's it."

"You don't shit where you eat, I get it."

"That girl told me she was twenty. She had a fake ID and everything. So, they had to drop the charges. I didn't prey on anyone."

The cops never came by to question me, so he could be telling the truth.

"You are careful," I accuse. "The ones who could fuck up your life think you're in love with them. They would never testify against you."

Court grins. It's a shit-eating grin. "If all of that were true, how would you feel about me?"

I think about the shitty things I've done. The horrible choices I've made. "I'm not judging."

"So, can we still be friends?" he asks.

"Is that what we are?" I turn towards my street.

"Yes, I think so."

"Cool, because I don't have any friends." I punch Court in the arm. "I need someone to throw me a baby shower."

"Do you still have the house to yourself?" He winks like a sleazeball. I know he's kidding, I'm too old for him.

I tell Court my mom is back and I don't feel like explaining our situation, so we go to his place. It's a shitty apartment a few blocks away. All of his windows face the back of other buildings.

"Why do you live in a box?"

Court hands me a glass of apple juice. "I'm a public school teacher with child support. I can't afford a view."

"Do you always keep apple juice in the house for your guests?"

"Ha. It's my daughter's. I only have that or beer, I figured in your condition you'd be better off with juice."

I take a sip. "It's good."

"It's organic crap her mother forces me to buy. She has her on this all-natural, non-GMO bullshit diet. I think she does it because she knows I can't afford it. It's just another way to fuck me."

"Well, you fucked her first," I remind him.

"That I did." Court knocks his beer bottle with my juice glass then takes a drink. "So, tell me about your baby-daddy situation."

I tell Court everything. *Everything*. Because it's Court and he doesn't judge. He won't think I'm a horrible person. If anyone understands bad choices, it's this guy.

"He raped you, Alee." Court walks to his shitty kitchen and tosses his empty bottle in a recycling bin. He opens the refrigerator and pulls out another beer. His anger surprises me. He seems concerned. Concerned is a good word to describe his emotional state. Concerned Court.

"No, it was just a really fucked-up situation. I let him take my pants off."

"You told him to stop and he didn't stop. That's rape."

"I guess if anyone would know, it's you," I joke.

Court doesn't think it's funny.

"You don't know Benny. We had a complicated relationship. Yes, he took advantage of me in a vulnerable situation. I don't know if I can call it rape. I definitely can't call him a rapist."

"He is. That fucking prick."

"You don't know him." *Why am I defending Benny?* I don't want Court to think I surround myself with completely fucked up people. Like him.

"So you wanted to fuck this guy. Fuck him in your fiancé's bed on the night of his funeral."

My throat gets stuck when he calls Laine my fiancé. I spin the ring on my finger and place my hand on my belly. Part of him is growing inside me. We're connected forever now.

Court sits beside me on his really uncomfortable IKEA couch. "What if this is Benny's baby." He places his hand on my leg. "What will you do then?"

I won't allow myself to consider it.

"It isn't."

"How do you know?"

249

"Because I say so."

"You can always get a blood test."

"Why would I do that?"

"To know for sure."

I don't want to know. I'll never know whose blood runs through this child's veins. It doesn't matter. In my heart, this is Laine's child.

SADIST

Chapter Thirty One

Mom's sobriety irks me. Yes, I'm happy she's sober but it's actually more stressful on me. I'm waiting for the hammer to drop. I come home from work every day holding my breath as I walk through the door. Who will she be? The mom who cooks organic meals and does yoga or the one who vomits in the trash and nearly burns down the house when she forgets the frozen pizza in the oven. It all boils down to trust. The only thing I trust is failure. It's a certainty in my life. Even Laine failed me. It's a shitty thing to believe, but he did. He joined the Marines. He left me, then he died. I won't be alone much longer. I'll have a little reminder of Laine and I'm going to helicopter parent that crap out of this kid. This baby is my reason for living.

The house smells like garlic and onions. Mom is making veggie lasagna for dinner. As soon as I walk into the kitchen, I realize I forgot to stop for bread.

"It smells delicious." I peek at the casserole dish over her shoulder. "Do I have time to go get the bread?"

"This needs to cool for about fifteen minutes. Don't bother going to the bakery, just run to Cala Foods."

I switch to my running shoes and grab my headphones. Heather is on my ass about pregnancy exercise. She teaches a Pilates class on the weekends and suddenly she's a health guru.

I stroll down the baby aisle at the grocery store. I'm practically a year away from needing anything from these shelves but it's fun to look. Once a man asked me a question about baby wipes. Me. Like I looked like someone who knew about baby wipes. About babies in general. I looked like a mother. My hand goes to my belly as I exit the aisle. *Soon.*

I grab two baguettes from the bakery and stand in the express line. My stomach grumbles. Nobody will mind if I munch a little bread while I wait. I am pregnant after all. I rip a chunk of bread from the top of the loaf and shove it in my mouth.

"Alee?"

I turn at the sound of Beverly's voice and force the bread down my throat. She asks how I'm doing and congratulates me on the baby.

"How did you find out?"

"I spoke to Janey the other day. She is over the moon about this baby." I move forward in line, she follows even though her basket carries more than the allotted fifteen items. "Have you told Benny yet?"

The bread threatens to make a reappearance. It would be kind of awesome to puke on Bev's fancy shoes. I look down at her feet. *Only a sadist wears six-inch heels to the grocery store.*

"Benny will be home this weekend. You two should get together. He'd love to see you."

I pretend I have to pee and step out of line before I say something horrible, like the truth. Bev offers to buy my bread.

"I changed my mind." I leave the partially eaten loaf on top of the candy rack and run out of the store.

***

On Saturday morning I wake up early and go for a walk. Mom likes to go with me, but I want to be alone today. I also want to stop for a donut. I'm enjoying a maple bar stuffed with bacon when Benny pulls beside me. I keep walking.

"Alee, please stop." His voice echoes into the empty street. It's too early for yelling. I don't want to make a scene. I stop. He walks up behind me and places his hand on my shoulder. I shrug it off.

"I don't want to talk to you."

253

"Then why did you stop?" Benny keeps a safe distance between us.

"When someone tells me to stop, I stop."

"I deserve that," he admits. "I deserve so much more." He reaches for me then pulls back. "I'm so sorry."

"You say that a lot. But sorry doesn't make it better. It doesn't make it go away."

"I know."

"I have to pee." I continue walking. Benny follows me, leaving his car parked crooked on the street.

"My mom told me about..." He pauses. "Is it mine?"

The noise I make is part anger, part cry, part pain. I walk faster.

"It's a valid question."

"If it were yours, then what?" I say to freak him out. He doesn't answer. He looks scared or sick. "It's Laine's." My throat constricts. It hurts that I can't say that with one hundred percent certainty.

"Are you sure the dates add up?"

"For the most part, yes."

Benny nods. "Okay, then. I mean, that's good news, right?" He isn't relieved the baby was fathered by Laine. He's disappointed.

254

Because I never say the right things or make good choices when it comes to Benny, I say, "What if the baby were yours. Would you want me to keep it?"

"Alee, I love you. If there is even a remote chance the baby is mine, it would make me the happiest man on earth."

Making Benny happy is the last thing I will ever do.

The next day Beverly calls. She asks me how many weeks along I am. When my due date is. I don't think Benny would tell anyone what happened between us. He said it himself, it was wrong. Does he really want Laine's family, his cousins, to know he had sex with me the night of Laine's funeral? When I ask Bev why she needs to know, she rattles on about planning a baby shower. The thought of being showered with gifts puts a little smile on my face.

"My friend from work already offered to host a shower for me, but thank you."

"It's normal to have more than one. Plus, Janey will be so excited to help in the planning."

I reluctantly agree and Bev says she'll get back to me in a few days with the details.

Two days later I'm served with a petition demanding a paternity test for my baby. I call Benny immediately.

"I'm sorry, Alee. But if that is my baby, I have a right to know."

"Does everyone have a right to know how the baby was conceived?"

Benny is silent for a few seconds. "We were drunk."

"Fuck you! You knew what you were doing," I cry. "I told you to stop." I lean against the front door and slide to the ground. "You want everyone to know what we did. They're going to hate me."

"This isn't about them. It's about my rights as a father."

"You will never be a father to my baby. Ever."

I hang up on him and walk to the kitchen. I pull a glass from the cabinet and fill it with water.

I won't have Benny's baby. I just won't.

A BAD TIME
TO BE SOBER
Chapter Thirty Two

My mother has been sober a year.

She traded bourbon for kale smoothies. She does yoga and runs around Lake Merced every Sunday morning, rain or shine. She is healed and I'm irrevocably broken.

I find her sitting at the dining room table. She is finishing her dinner juice when I pull out the chair across from her. She smiles curiously. We never eat dinner together; we don't do anything together. Not for her lack of trying.

"What's going on?"

Her smile fades when I slide a glass of bourbon in front of her. I don't want to lose the element of surprise so I quickly tell her my plan. Before she can fully comprehend what is happening, I hand her a list of things to do after I go to my room.

"I set up Netflix so you can catch up on your shows. I also put a pill in the drawer next to your jewelry box. It will help you sleep."

Mom scans the list then looks at the glass of bourbon. Her hair is pulled into a low ponytail, streaks of gray pinstripe the top of her head. I remember when her hair was so black it looked purple in certain light. Her face and skin still carry a youthful tone, more so now that she's healthy. The older I get, the more I look like her. I'll die before I turn into my mother.

"I set your alarm for six," I continue. "Here is the phone number for Duggan's funeral home on Valencia. Call them first thing to set up an appointment."

She looks from the list to the bourbon glass again. When she's sober, there is no liquor in the house. I bought this a week ago and hid it in my room.

"Is this some kind of test to see if I'll drink?" She pushes the glass away. "Because I'm better now, Alee." I can tell from the desperate look in her eyes that she really wants to believe that.

"No." I walk to the kitchen to give her a moment to process what I'm saying. I don't want to rile her up or get lured into a fight.

"Alee, this is crazy—" She stops herself. "I mean, this isn't rational thinking. You know how you get when you start to feel sad. Are you taking the meds?"

I hate when she brings up my depression like it's something a pill can cure. It's part of my DNA, it's who I am. I don't want to be this person anymore.

She says she cares. I tell her it isn't enough. It's never been enough. I tell her she checked out on me a long time ago. I want to hurt her. It works. She takes a sip of bourbon. Savoring the feeling as it slips past her lips into her juice-filled stomach.

"How do you plan on doing it?" she asks, as if she's just playing along.

"Drugs."

"What kind?" She thinks I'm full of shit now. She knows I would never do drugs. I don't even drink.

"Bad kind."

"Where did you get them?"

I won't tell her I got the drugs from the same dealer who supplied my father. She doesn't know I found him. He found me.

"Does it really matter where they came from?"

She begins to cry and I think of the time she showed up for my parent-teacher conference drunk. Painful memories fuel my intentions.

"What about me?" Mom sobs.

"What about you?" I tack a little extra sass on the end. As much as I try to hate my mother, I can't stand to see her cry.

She looks at her hands. "I'll be alone."

"You're already alone. You haven't loved anyone since *he* left."

Her eyes bounce to the bottle on the table. She doesn't argue. She knows I'm right.

"So, you're just going to get up, walk to your room, and that's it." She wipes her face with the back of her hand, then grips the glass in front of her.

"I'm going to get up, turn off the coffee pot, say, 'Goodnight, Mom,' and then go to my room."

I don't give her a time. If I do, she'll hold me to it. If things get bad and I want to go to my room early, she'll protest. If things go long and I'm late, she'll see it as hope.

"*Goodnight, Mom?* Those will be the last words you say to me?"

Out of everything I've told her, this is her main concern. Coming up with last words wasn't on my to-do list. I'm sure I could think of something more appropriate if she were a different mom. The kind of mom they write Hallmark cards about.

"Is there something else you want me to say?" It's difficult to hold back my irritation.

She thinks for a full two minutes. She doesn't drink from her glass or look at me; she just sits and thinks. When she finally tries to speak, her voice cracks. "Say that poem you wrote. You know, the one from third grade."

"What poem?"

"You wrote me a poem for Valentine's Day on the back of a pink heart with white lace on the front. It hung on the fridge for a long time. I used to read it every day."

"How did it go?" I indulge her.

"Roses are red. Violets are blue. If I had to pick one, I'd choose you."

"I don't remember writing that."

"You did. It was third grade. You had Mrs. Jordan."

Wait. I didn't make a Valentine's card in third grade. I was absent that week with chickenpox. The heart she's referring to was given to me. By what's-his-name. He had a Ninja Turtles backpack. I look at my mother's melancholy face. She's waiting for me to say something about the stupid poem.

"Okay. I'll say the poem."

"Thank you." She lifts her glass and takes a drink.

The last words I speak on this earth won't even be mine. The irony. Only my mother would care more about a poem than stopping me. Shouldn't she call someone? Or at the very least tell me I'm wrong? Tell me there's something to live for? A good mother would. Not mine. I watch her pour another glass.

"Pour me one."

"Really?"

"Yes. I don't have to worry about my liver. Unless you donate my organs."

"Oh God, no." She walks to the china cabinet and gets a glass. Her words are slippery, and her eyes are crooked. Good. Drunk mom will slip into a coma, and when she wakes, I'll be gone. She sits down, pours my drink, and slides it across the table. She lifts her glass to me. We clink them together.

"Did we just toast to my death?"

She chokes and sets her glass down. "No! I just...I don't know." She shakes her head back and forth. "I don't know why I did that. It just felt right."

I know what she means. We're sharing our first mother-daughter moment in a very long time. Something that wouldn't be happening if I was going to be here in the morning. *Is that what it takes to get her to care?* It takes some effort to keep my tears at bay. I want to cry, or laugh, or scream. This is my last day on Earth; I should be allowed to express any emotion I damn well please.

"What time are you going to bed?" She drains the rest of her glass.

I don't answer. I go to the kitchen and begin making coffee.

"What was the last thing you ate?" she asks from the dining room.

I think about it for a second. "I ate two blueberry waffles this morning. With butter, no syrup."

"That's your last meal?"

"I guess." I shrug and slide the coffee pot into its place. I like the symmetry of the coffee maker. Everything fits perfectly together. If one component is off, nothing works.

"Do you still like spaghetti?"

Seriously? She doesn't even know if I like spaghetti.

"Doesn't everyone?"

Her chair scrapes the hardwood floor, a few seconds later her slippers shuffle into the kitchen. "I'll make you spaghetti."

I move away from the counter and allow her to pull a pot from the cabinet by my knees. She fills it with water and sets it on the stove. I place a lid on the top.

"It boils faster that way," I tell her.

She nods with a sad smile then opens the refrigerator. My mother browns meat and crushes tomatoes. She spices and tastes. I watch her the way I did when I was little before my father left. When things were normal. We liked normal. He didn't. Sitting down for a meal with his wife and child was torture for him. That's why he left. He was flawed, not us. I hope she knows that.

We return to the dining room with our plates and a bag of sliced white bread. We eat in silence. At one point she pulls out a piece of bread, butters it, and hands it to me. The thought of eating cold butter normally makes me gag, but I eat it. I eat the whole damn thing.

When we're finished, she takes our plates to the sink and turns on the water.

"Don't do those now," I tell her. "Save them for tomorrow. You'll need something to do."

Her shoulders slump and she turns the water off. "I should have done this more often. I shouldn't have let you raise yourself. I failed you." She falls to her knees and sobs against the cabinet door.

I watch my mother cry for me. For herself. For the life we didn't have. I don't go to her. I don't comfort her. I don't know how.

PICTURE PRISON

Chapter Thirty Three

Mom wants to look at pictures. Pictures and booze go hand in hand. These old photos are little time machines to moments she travels back to in her mind. She feels the cool air as the fog settles over a photo of her and my father at Twin Peaks. She smells the hot sidewalk in her favorite picture of me riding my bike in front of the house.

She pulls out the blue albums with gold foil trim and sets them on the dining room table. They're filled with pictures of my mother's childhood and some of my parents before I was born. The pictures of me stop at age five. That's when the camera was replaced with a bottle of bourbon. I know where each one was taken and the explanation behind it. She insists on telling the stories anyway.

"This one was Christmas 1992. Right after I took this picture, you spilled hot chocolate all over your new dress."

"I know," I say with a yawn. "I've seen all of these, Mom. I don't want to relive my childhood."

The photos are a lie. Nobody took pictures of the fights, the crying, the leaving. The only honest thing about them is their location. This house hasn't changed in twenty years. Besides the paint, everything is the same. The dining room table, the rug in the hall. The sofa.

Countless nights I watched my mother sleep, her mouth open, drooling into the sofa cushions. The same ones Laine made love to me on the day we conceived our baby.

"Look at this one." She points to a photo of me and my father sitting on the porch. I'm wearing shorts over a frilly pink bathing suit. "This was the hottest day of 1994. It reached—"

"One hundred and three," I interrupt. "I know."

Reminiscing isn't going to change my mind. The albums aren't going to save my life. If anything, they reinforce my decision. The smell of old photos brings me back to the nights my mother sat at this table crying into her bourbon glass. Crying for a life that only exists in her mind.

That is what I am trying to avoid. She turns the page and relives the captured moments trapped in the plastic sleeves of these albums. She only exists in these memories. I close the album in front of me and look at the dusty chandelier above the dining room table. I have an unhealthy attachment to the mismatched bulbs, the spice rack, the sofa—anything Laine touched.

Mom wipes a tear from her face. She knows why I love the light bulbs. Why I won't let her buy a new couch. She knows I can't live another day without him. "I have something for you."

She leaves and I check my phone. It's eight-forty-five I don't want to waste any more time on pictures, but what else is there to do with my mother? We have nothing in common. That isn't true. We suffer from the same pain and loss. My father, Laine. The lives we could've had, but didn't fight for.

She returns to the table and sets a large manila envelope in front of me. My name is printed on a white label affixed to the front. The return address reads RW Photography. I flip over the envelope and find it's never been opened. My throat constricts to hold in the scream begging to escape. I turn it over again and notice there is no postage, which means it was delivered to the house.

"How long have you hid this from me?" The question comes out louder than I expected. Mom jumps slightly.

"A few months after."

"Why are you giving it to me now?" I bite my cheek to keep from exploding. "Why now, after all this time?"

Her reply is interrupted by tears. She doesn't try to speak through them.

I run my hand along the envelope. "Do you know what's in here?"

She nods. "Yes, she came by in person to deliver them. You had just gone back to work." She pauses to sip her drink, then lets out a long sigh to gain her composure. "You were just getting better; I didn't want to set you back."

"Set me back!" I slam my hand on the table and jump out of my chair. My mother recoils as if I'm going to hit her. I would never hurt her physically, not when mental abuse is so much more effective.

"I was drowning, Mom! I could barely get out of bed in the morning and you had the one thing that could possibly pull me out. A life preserver to bring me a fucking ounce of happiness, and you kept it from me!" Tears roll down my cheek, into my mouth. I swallow them. "I hate you for this!" I grab the envelope and run to my room.

I lay the photos across my bed. There are forty-two of them. She snapped the first one as we walked into the plaza. We're tiny specs in a wide shot of birds in flight. In each photo we get larger and closer. The photo of Laine kneeling takes my breath away. I will never be that happy again. There are sequential shots of Laine placing the ring on my finger, then standing up. My favorite is the pause before he takes me in his arms. If time travel were real, this is the moment I would go back to. Even if I couldn't change the outcome of our lives. Even if I had to relive every horrible event that comes after. I would endure them all again for that one moment.

"Alee, please don't do this," Mom cries from the hall. She tries to open the door. It's locked.

I had a new, stronger lock installed two weeks ago. The old one could be popped open with a butter knife. This one is a deadbolt.

"Alee, I promise things will be different. I'll be better. I'm trying. Give me more time."

Her words don't matter. Nothing matters.

She pounds on the door, the wall, the floor. There's pounding coming from all sides. I pull my pillow off the bed, careful not to disrupt the timeline of photos. I lie on the floor and place the pillow over my head.

"I messed up. I know I did. But I've been trying to make it up to you. I want to be there for you. Please give me one more chance!" She's crying hysterically. She's never cried for me. This is her last chance.

NO HAPPY ENDINGS

Chapter Thirty Four

I check the stash in my bottom drawer. The pills, the Nyquil, the bag of white powder, the balloon full of heroin, and the syringe. A piece of cotton, a spoon, and a lighter from the junk drawer in the kitchen. Everything is ready. All I have to do is calm my mother down. I see now she's going to be a problem.

This was a good test run. I didn't plan for her outburst. I need concentration when I prepare the contents going into the syringe. I've only done it a few dozen times. Jesus let me practice prepping his high. He said I'm good enough. I mean, it isn't like I want it to be perfect. Junkies are only careful so they don't accidentally kill themselves. I don't have to worry about that.

I close the drawer and compose myself before opening the door. My mother is sitting on the floor holding her cell phone. I don't believe she will actually call anyone. Mom was never there for me, she's never given me anything, not even her love. This is why I told her about my plan. I know she won't stop me. In some sick way, honoring my wishes gives her a chance to do something right by me, even if I'm wrong.

I step around her and go to the kitchen. I pull a mug from the cabinet and pour myself a cup of coffee. She walks in when I open the refrigerator.

"We're out of creamer. I meant to buy some today. I forgot." She pours herself of a cup.

This bothers me immensely. I have to drink my coffee with creamer. I close the door harder than necessary. I was really looking forward to having my final cup of coffee.

"I'll get some in the morning." She sips her black coffee and glares at me over the rim.

"Can you be any more of a bitch?"

"Nothing I do or say will stop you, so." She shrugs and walks out of the kitchen. She's trying to pull some reverse psychology on me. Like her wanting me to do it will make me not want to. It's so juvenile. So petty. So effective.

I follow her to the dining room and watch her stack the photo albums into a pile. She carries them back to their shelf

271

in the hall closet. I wait in the dining room for her to return. She doesn't. She goes to the living room and sits on the sofa clutching her mug like she can't wait to be rid of me. I can hurt her. I want to hurt her. I walk into the living room and sit on the opposite side of the couch. The fog has rolled in; we can't even see across the street. We're enveloped in a dank, dense cloud of pain.

"I saw my father," I say to the window, as if it has been waiting to hear those words for twenty years.

She sucks in a breath.

"I ran into him at BART a few years ago." I'll let her believe he's normal. Like I saw him on his way to work, not to shoot up in the park.

"He's alive?" She tries to hide the angst in her voice. It doesn't work.

"Yep," I say, but I don't know if it's true. He could've killed himself or overdosed, by now. "We used to meet every Thursday."

I see her eyes calculating all the Thursdays I came home late.

"Used to? You don't meet anymore?" Her tone is arrogant like she already knows he bailed. I won't give her the satisfaction of being right.

"He moved to Portland." It will hurt her most to believe he is healthy and happy living without her. That he doesn't want her. That's my revenge.

The bourbon bottle is empty. It's almost ten. Ten was my deadline. My expiration. I think now that ten is too early. I warm up a plate of spaghetti. Just the noodles, no sauce. I toss a tiny slab of butter in the bowl then put it in the microwave for one minute. When it begins to crackle and pop, I open the door. I remove the bowl and take it to the dining room table. I douse the noodles with parmesan cheese and I eat.

"What are you doing?" Mom asks from the living room.

"I'm eating," I say with a mouthful of pasta. I swipe to open my phone and make my social media rounds, checking Facebook first. I don't have very many friends; the ones I do have are mostly through Laine. The few people who friend requested me from high school, I declined. These are the same girls who wrote slut on my locker. Now they want to be my friend. Like all the horrible things they said no longer matter.

News flash: it does.

I close the Facebook app and click on Instagram. I scroll through the usual posts of food and selfies. I'm slurping another forkful of noodles when I see it. I choke and drop my fork.

It's a black and white picture, the same one I had taped to the wall beside my bucket list. There are fifty-two comments on the picture. All *congrats* with the baby head emoji.

Motherfucker.

COUNTING SHEEP
Chapter Thirty Five

I set my laptop on the dining room table. I can't angry-type on a cell phone. I need my full keyboard. I log in to Facebook and click his picture, then click *message*, and stare at the blank box contemplating what I want to say. I have conversations with him all the time. I yell obscenities at him. I curse him. I cry to him. These discussions are all one-sided because they only exist in my mind. I have not seen or spoken to Benny in a year.

I type one word: Hi.

The rest sort of flows out in a blur:

I saw Misty's post. You get to have your baby after all. Asshole.

I hit enter to move to the next line and the message is gone. It now appears as a blue bubble on the screen.

"NO!" I yell. Followed by, "Fuck fuck fuck."

How do I get it back? I can't get it back! I uncheck the stupid little option that says *press enter to send. Fuck you, Facebook.*

Mom walks into the dining room. "What's wrong?"

I don't answer because suddenly the date and time appear under the blue bubble.

No! He's reading the message.

"Everything is wrong, Mother." I'm heavy on the word mother. "I accidentally sent Benny a message on Facebook." Mom doesn't know what happened between me and Benny. As far as I know, only Beverly knows. I made sure of that.

The little bouncing circles start to roll in place. The next thing I know, Benny's picture pops onto the screen.

Alee, I'm so happy you reached out. I think about you all the time. I'm sorry you had to find out like that. I thought about calling. I was right, you still hate me.

At least he's perceptive.

The bubbles start to bounce again. I realize that he knows I've seen his message. *Fucking Facebook.* I'm about to close the window when his bubble head pops up.

I miss Laine every day. I really wish we could've missed him together.

My fingers fly across the keyboard.

You ruined any chance of us missing him together.

His next message asks if he can call me. I reply no.

I need to see you, Alee.

Benny Calderon is the last person I want to see. He is the last voice I want to hear.

He is the last.

I ask him if he's in New York.

I'm home for the weekend. Can I come over?

Perfect. This is perfect.

Benny arrives at eleven fifteen. My mother goes to her room with a promise not to say anything about my plans. I let her think Benny coming over means I changed my mind. She's wrong. Benny is the missing link. The last piece of my puzzle.

I open the door and step back to allow him inside, he doesn't try to hug me, we barely make eye contact. He looks older, tired. He smells the same.

"I'm so glad you agreed to see me." He sits on the sofa holding an envelope. "You look good."

I sit on the opposite end of the couch. "How's doctor stuff?"

"Exhausting. I'm in a three-year program so it's non-stop. But I like it. It keeps me busy. Focused."

"How's Misty?" I roll my eyes because I can't say her name without wanting to make a gag sound.

"She's still annoying as ever."

"Do you love her?"

"Not like I love you." He didn't say loved, as in past tense. Benny still loves me. Even after all the horrible things we've done to each other. "Why did you invite me over?" He looks hopeful, like I'm going to make all of his dreams come true. Sick fuck.

"We never talked after the baby..."

His eyes drop to the floor and he clears his throat. "It's okay, Alee. You don't need to apologize. I shouldn't have pushed so hard for the paternity test before the baby was born. I should've waited. My mother said it was safe." His disdain for Beverly gives me a small iota of pleasure. It almost makes me second guess my confession.

There is only one person who knows the truth: Bryn's mom, Frances. I needed someone to drive me home. I called her the night before, told her what I was planning. She didn't even ask why.

"I'm sorry about the Facebook message. It was immature for me to say that about your baby."

"That's okay. Believe me, this baby wasn't planned." He sits back and runs his hand down his face.

"I thought you really wanted to be a father."

Benny looks at me. Like, *really* looks at me. His eyes are dark, and not just because he has circles under them. When he finally speaks, his voice is low, childlike almost.

"I wanted to be the father of your baby." He reaches for my hand. I let him take it. "I can't stop loving you. I never will." He holds my hand to his lips, closes his eyes prayer-like. My timing couldn't be more perfect. Benny is vulnerable, easy to hurt. I always thought I'd carry this secret to my grave. Benny deserves to know.

The next words out of my mouth are harsh. So harsh that I've never said them aloud to anyone. Not even Court.

"I killed our baby."

Benny's eyes flick open. Wide-open.

"I did it on purpose because I didn't want to have your child. When I found out the baby wasn't Laine's I knew there was no way I would love it the way a mother should."

Secrecy was a condition of doing the paternity test. Beverly and Benny promised they wouldn't tell the Dicaros there was a chance Benny could have fathered my baby. None of us wanted to inflict that pain on Laine's family. They'd been through enough. When the results of the paternity test came back with bad news, I wanted them to

279

hear it from me. That conversation never happened. It wasn't needed after my trip to the clinic. I made it clear to Benny and Beverly that I never wanted to hear from them again. They've held up their end of the deal. I never imagined I'd be the one who reached out to him.

"Why are you telling me this now?" He squeezes the envelope in his hand.

"After all the horrible things we've said about each other—the lies, the truths—I guess I just wanted you to know who I really am." I stand and walk towards my room, leaving Benny on the sofa. I stop in front of my mother's door. I place my hand on the outside and I quietly recite the poem.

"Roses are red, violets are blue. If I had to choose one, I'd choose you."

"Alee? Are you okay?" Benny stands at the end of the hall watching me.

"Yes, finally."

He holds out the envelope in his hand. "I have something for you it's from…"

His words are silenced by my bedroom door. The deadbolt locks into place. I hope it lives up to its name. I remove the items from my bottom drawer and arrange them on the dresser. I lay the pink Converse socks and the bucket list beside them. I take the pills first, washing them down with the Nyquil. It tastes bad. Really bad. I fight to keep from vomiting. I immediately start to prepare the needle, remembering the afternoons watching Jesus. Warming the spoon, soaking the cotton. When it's ready, I fill the syringe and sit on my bed. The effects of the pills and the Nyquil are already making me woozy. I'm such a lightweight, this should be easy. I wrap the belt around my arm and tighten it… a knock breaks my concentration.

"Alee," Benny says. "I have a letter…"

I find the vein, the one Jesus said was my good one; it's plump and ready. With a shaky hand, I place the needle against my skin. I hear my mother in the hall. She asks Benny what is happening. He tells her he isn't sure. She cries my name and tells him to call for help. She pounds on my door begging me to stop. *To wait. To live.*

I pierce my skin with the needle and press the plunger.

The pounding is stronger, Benny pleads for me to let him in as I empty the needle into my vein.

It falls to the floor.

The drugs move quickly.

I lay back on my bed.

I stare at my ceiling.

I count sheep until the banging stops.

JUST IN CASE

Chapter Thirty Six

LAINE

Personally, I think it's bad luck to write one of these things but the guys are giving me a lot of shit. Hell, one dude wrote a letter to his last three girlfriends. Alee deserves more than words written on flimsy notebook paper. What I have to say should be forged in stone. My girl deserves blood, not ink.

I click open the pen and test it on the corner of the paper. *Blue ink.* Alee's favorite color. Maybe that's a sign. I never believed in fate or destiny until that day in the coffee shop. It wasn't the first time I 'accidentally' ran into her. That day was particularly shitty and I needed a reason to smile.

An hour before I sat on a stool beside my best friend's girl, my parents told me they couldn't afford to send me to college. It wasn't like I grew up poor or anything. Our house is worth close to a mil. We vacationed every summer, and I even went to ski camp in Tahoe. By most standards, I had a privileged childhood. I did everything right: got the grades, played ball, and stayed away from the bad shit. What did I get in return? The promise of a city job. Busting my ass every day for the next forty years fixing broken water mains. *Thanks, but no thanks.* The jokes on me because that shitty job never came through. I've wasted the last three years waiting to live a life I didn't want. Enlisting was the first thing I have ever done for me. That's not true. The first thing I ever did for me was kissing Alee. When she kissed me back, I just about busted in my jeans. She was—is—the most beautiful thing in my life. Even when she wasn't mine, Alee made everything around her brighter, which is ironic, because she lives her life in darkness. I hope, no, I pray, she finds something to illuminate her while I'm gone.

Alee is my country, my honor, my savior. She is what I fight for. In this life and the next. We're linked forever, light and dark. One doesn't exist without the other. There is no positive without a negative. No loss without hope. How do I tell Alee any of this in a letter? A letter she will never read. I have no plans to die. Not today. Not anytime soon.

Just in case. My ass. Negative thinking gets you killed. Hell, writing this letter could trigger a chain of events that leads to my demise. So, why am I sitting here, staring at the wall, when they're watching *Forest Gump* in the rec room?

Just in case.

Just in case something happens, I need her to know she'll be all right. I want her to know how much I loved her. How she saved me.

How can I convey my feelings in a letter? Words in real life hold power. Meaning. Feeling. Words on paper are just words. I never allow myself to think about the what if's and just in cases. I'm not afraid of dying. I'm scared as hell of what my death will do to Alee. She doesn't realize her strength is in her fragility. She's been on the brink of falling apart so many times, yet she always finds a way to hold on. I had a dream about her once. She was standing on a crumbling ledge. As pieces fell around her, she maintained balance. I tried to throw her a rope, but it turned out to be a vine-covered in thorns. Blood ran down her arms as the thorns ripped through her skin. She looked up at me, perched in safety and said, "Thanks a lot, Laine."

I woke to find her sleeping soundly beside me. That was the night before I left for SOI. The next morning, I found out she lost our baby. After SOI, I realized how much I needed her. *Needed purpose.* Alee's life hasn't been easy, but she continues to muscle through it. She can handle so much

more than she even knows. That's what I need to tell her.
What she will need to hear just in case I don't come back.

Dear Alee,

Make life your bitch.

Yours forever,

Laine

THANK YOU

I don't know who to thank first. So many amazing people took the time to read and critique every draft of this story. I set out to write a book as emotionally charged as Thizz. I hope I've accomplished that with Alee.

Murphy Rae: The cover of this book is stunning and the feedback of the first draft helped guide me in a completely different direction, cause it was crap.

Rachel: I forced you to read this twice and both times I drank gin while waiting for you to finish. I'll take your spoiled eyes over fresh eyes any day.

Tracy Finlay: If it wasn't for you this book wouldn't have a plot. Wait, does it even have a plot now? No matter. You introduced me to the Plot Clock and changed my life forever.

Laura Hull (Red Pen Princess): You put the cherry on top of this book.

Cindy: If it wasn't for you, this book wouldn't exist.

Ali: This is my favorite book I've written. I'm not saying you're my favorite. Your sister did try to kill me though.

Achilles: You survived another book. Good dog.

My group: I heart you all so much.

SUICIDE WARM LINE: 415.421.1880

Don't wait until it's too late. Contact the Warm Line, a peer-run support line.

Chat online at www.mentalhealthsf.org

National Suicide Prevention Lifeline 1-800-273-8255

National Sexual Assault Hotline 1-800-656-4673

Date Rape is forced sexual assault or rape by a known romantic interest or date involving sex you don't agree to.

25% of the reported date rapes are committed by someone very close to the victim, such as a current or ex-boyfriend or girlfriend, or even an ex-spouse.

Safe sexual relations that involve consent are:

Agreed-upon. Both parties agree to and respect each other's boundaries.

Considerate. Approved of and enjoyed by each person.

Trusting. Individuals can depend on the honesty of the other person.

Nonviolent. Never done with intent of harm.

It is not consent if there is:

Doubt. You did not specifically give consent.

Disrespect. Your partner ignores your boundaries.

Fear. You are afraid to say "no."

Intimidation. You say "yes" to avoid conflict or harm.

ABOUT ME

Nicole lives in Northern California with her family, including her dog, Achilles. She is an avid gin drinker and lover of donuts. In addition to writing books, she has won her fantasy football league twice.

Instagram: @nicoleloufas
Facebook Group: Nicole's Book Rehab
Facbook Page: Nicole Loufas, Author
Twitter: @nicoleloufas

Other books:
Thizz, A Love Story
Illusion of Ecstasy, next dose in the Thizz series
The Lunam Ceremony
The Lunam Deception
The Lunam Legacy
Got Mine, Men of Trance book 1
Side Game, Men of Trance, book 2
The Excursion, a vacation novella
Scarlett, an Every Woman novella